TREES WITHOUT WIND

WEATHERHEAD BOOKS ON ASIA

WEATHERHEAD EAST ASIAN INSTITUTE, COLUMBIA UNIVERSITY

WEATHERHEAD BOOKS ON ASIA

WEATHERHEAD EAST ASIAN INSTITUTE, COLUMBIA UNIVERSITY

LITERATURE

David Der-wei Wang, Editor

Ye Zhaoyan, *Nanjing 1937: A Love Story*, translated by Michael Berry (2003)

Oda Makoto, *The Breaking Jewel*, translated by Donald Keene (2003)

Han Shaogong, *A Dictionary of Maqiao*, translated by Julia Lovell (2003)

Takahashi Takako, *Lonely Woman*, translated by Maryellen Toman Mori (2004)

Chen Ran, *A Private Life*, translated by John Howard-Gibbon (2004)

Eileen Chang, *Written on Water*, translated by Andrew F. Jones (2004)

Writing Women in Modern China: The Revolutionary Years, 1936–1976, edited by Amy D. Dooling (2005)

Han Bangqing, *The Sing-song Girls of Shanghai*, first translated by Eileen Chang, revised and edited by Eva Hung (2005)

Loud Sparrows: Contemporary Chinese Short-Shorts, translated and edited by Aili Mu, Julie Chiu, and Howard Goldblatt (2006)

Hiratsuka Raichō, *In the Beginning, Woman Was the Sun*, translated by Teruko Craig (2006)

Zhu Wen, I Love Dollars *and Other Stories of China*, translated by Julia Lovell (2007)

Kim Sowŏl, *Azaleas: A Book of Poems,* translated by David McCann (2007)

Wang Anyi, *The Song of Everlasting Sorrow: A Novel of Shanghai*, translated by Michael Berry with Susan Chan Egan (2008)

Ch'oe Yun, *There a Petal Silently Falls: Three Stories by Ch'oe Yun*, translated by Bruce and Ju-Chan Fulton (2008)

Inoue Yasushi, *The Blue Wolf: A Novel of the Life of Chinggis Khan*, translated by Joshua A. Fogel (2009)

Anonymous, *Courtesans and Opium: Romantic Illusions of the Fool of Yangzhou*, translated by Patrick Hanan (2009)

Cao Naiqian, *There's Nothing I Can Do When I Think of You Late at Night*, translated by John Balcom (2009)

Park Wan-suh, *Who Ate Up All the Shinga? An Autobiographical Novel*, translated by Yu Young-nan and Stephen J. Epstein (2009)

Yi T'aejun, *Eastern Sentiments*, translated by Janet Poole (2009)

Hwang Sunwŏn, *Lost Souls: Stories*, translated by Bruce and Ju-Chan Fulton (2009)

Kim Sŏk-pŏm, *The Curious Tale of Mandogi's Ghost*, translated by Cindy Textor (2010)

Xiaomei Chen, editor, *The Columbia Anthology of Modern Chinese Drama* (2011)

(continued on p. 188)

LI RUI

TREES WITHOUT WIND

A NOVEL

TRANSLATED BY JOHN BALCOM

COLUMBIA UNIVERSITY PRESS

NEW YORK

This publication has been supported by the
Richard W. Weatherhead Publication Fund of the
Weatherhead East Asian Institute, Columbia University.

COLUMBIA UNIVERSITY PRESS
Publishers Since 1893
NEW YORK   CHICHESTER, WEST SUSSEX

Library of Congress Cataloging-in-Publication Data
Li, Rui, 1950-
[Wu feng zhi shu. English]
Trees without wind : a novel / Li Rui ; translated by John Balcom.
p.   cm. — (Weatherhead Books on Asia)
ISBN 978-0-231-16274-6 (cloth) — ISBN 978-0-231-16275-3 (pbk.) —
ISBN 978-0-231-53104-7 (electronic)
I. Balcom, John. II. Title.
PL2877.R85W7813   2012
895.1'352—dc23

2012014231

LI RUI'S MASTERFUL NOVEL *Trees Without Wind* is set against the backdrop of the Great Proletarian Cultural Revolution (1966–76), or Mao's last revolution, as it is termed by some today. For ten years China was thrown into utter chaos as Mao unleashed the Red Guard to once again consolidate his political power and to implement a reign of perpetual revolution. A younger generation of extreme idealists sought to carry forward Chairman Mao's plans while aiming to overthrow the status quo. Mao possessed near divine status and was venerated in a cult of personality that would have disastrous consequences for the country. Li Rui sees the decade as the most important, if not the defining period in modern Chinese history.

Li Rui is an important member of that generation of fine writers who lived through the Cultural Revolution and came to prominence in the 1980s. He was born in Beijing in 1950 and grew up there. In 1969, after finishing secondary school, he was sent to the Shanxi countryside, where he worked as a peasant for six years, followed by another three years as a steel-mill worker. His parents died during this time, and his siblings were scattered around China. Li Rui's experience in the countryside during the Cultural Revolution was formative to his development as a writer. Much of his fictional output has been concerned with rural Shanxi in that tumultuous period.

The novel grew out of the author's short story "A Funeral," which is included in his 1989 short-story collection *The Earth*. Four years later, Li Rui revisited this piece and decided it needed further development. Over the next three years, he worked at surpassing his earlier efforts as a writer to produce something totally new in terms of form and narrative style. He sought to bring the Cultural Revolution, which had served as an ill-defined backdrop to his work, into sharper focus, feeling that the period was key to understanding China and had an importance to the Chinese similar to that of the two world wars for Europeans. Published in 1996, *Trees Without Wind* offers a view of the Cultural Revolution from the hindsight of twenty years.

In China, Li Rui's fiction is often lumped with the "root-seeking" school of modern Chinese writing, which was largely concerned with an examination of rural life and values. This categorization is due in large part to his early collections of short stories, which are set in the countryside. In *Trees Without Wind*, the setting is a remote village in the Luliang Mountains of Shanxi Province, a particularly poor and backward region. In the tradition of Zhao Shuli, the great proletarian novelist from Shanxi, who is remembered for his use of dialect to create a new written language to represent peasant speech, Li Rui utilizes the regional speech of Shanxi to further heighten the verisimilitude of his characters. Because Li Rui has chosen to write about a poor province, using the local language, his writing has sometimes been dismissed by Chinese critics as a throwback to an earlier time—an oversimplification, to be sure.

Depicted in the novel are the political movements and in-fighting of the period, replete with the obligatory quotations from Chairman Mao. Yesterday's discourse of power now seems a relic. Alongside the official language of power, Li Rui juxtaposes Shanxi peasant speech. Yet both this bygone language of power and the rural dialect are contained within extreme formal innovations that include multiple perspectives, stream-of-consciousness-narrative, and flashbacks. With consummate artistry, Li Rui dissects and deconstructs the Cultural Revolution, exposing it for what it was: a cultural, social, and economic disaster. The novel also upends the genre of revolutionary fiction in terms of content and form. The linear plots, the black-and-white purity of values, and the absence of complex or middle characters that typify such writing are all undermined here. Life becomes ambiguous, human motives are hypocritical and self-serving, values are impure, and the good guys don't always win.

The character Zhang Weiguo best embodies the metanarrative of the Cultural Revolution. Zhang's own idealism and desire to be a writer have been inspired and shaped by proletarian fiction and movies of the revolution. He seeks to imitate one proletarian writer in particular, not just in going to the countryside to change the world but also in his very appearance, by adopting the same black-rimmed glasses worn by his model. Since arriving in Stunted Flats, Zhang has kept a diary, which is actually a work of revolutionary fiction based on his experiences. Throughout the novel, there is a frequent blurring of fiction and reality in Zhang Weiguo's references to his fictional alter ego, Zhang Yingjie. While the fictional protagonist struggles to realize his ideals, Zhang Weiguo is far more complex. Even as he interprets

his own motives through the metanarrative of the party idealism of the Cultural Revolution, his actual behavior is, ironically,
much more ambiguous. He compromises his ideals to make deals
with the locals to undermine the authority of an older cadre.

The complex social and political relationships in the village
and the various levels of irony are inseparable from the novel's
form. The novel is narrated from the perspectives of a dozen
characters, one of whom is a donkey who thinks in terms of
color association—therefore, in her monologues, the "green
one" refers to her caretaker, Uncle Gimpy, who feeds her, and so
on. Much of the irony arises from the multiple perspectives, as
events are interpreted in different ways by different characters,
and in the gap between self-perception and perception by others. Irony is also a product of intertextuality, of reading the
novel within the tradition of modern Chinese fiction, especially
in its later revolutionary manifestation, in which plots and characters were often flattened as writers sought to portray workers,
peasants, and soldiers as heroes. For example, the struggle ses-
sion against the sole class enemy in the village takes on a particularly ironic twist when read against, say, other struggle ses-
sions depicted in a classic of proletarian fiction such as Ding
Ling's *The Sun Shines on the Sanggang River.* The revolution has
become a caricature of itself.

This artistic synthesis achieved by Li Rui is symptomatic of
the milieu in which he wrote. China, having rejected the excesses
of the Cultural Revolution, had embarked upon economic re-
forms on a massive scale and had opened to the West, in the wake
of which came great social and cultural change and demands for
greater political liberalization. During the 1980s and 1990s China
was exposed to twentieth-century literary trends and schools

from around the world, through both translations and academic studies. Modernist writing, previously considered decadent and available only to a select few of the Party elite during the Cultural Revolution, was suddenly widely available and came as a shock, providing inspiration and a fertilizing influence. For example, Li Wenjun's translations of Faulkner's fiction in the 1980s were an important source of inspiration for Li Rui. Faulkner, especially the author of *As I Lay Dying*, is an abiding presence behind the novel. The result is a masterful blend of regional content and high modernist style.

The title of *Trees Without Wind* refers to a Chinese expression: "the tree may prefer calm, but the wind will not subside." As Director Liu, one of the characters in the novel, explains its significance within the revolutionary context: "It means the tree wants to stop and rest, but the wind blows and blows, and even if the tree wants to stop, it can't; even if it wants to stand still, it can't. That's the way class struggle is, no one has a choice—you might not want to struggle, but you have to!" Class struggle and revolution are proclaimed as independent of human will, though they are depicted as something far different in the novel. The villagers of Stunted Flats all yearn to be free of the buffeting winds of revolution. Ironically, they generally think that life was better without all the upheavals caused by the self-interested officials and ideologues and their games. (The juxtaposition of life in the village during the Cultural Revolution with the brutality under the Japanese during the 1930s and '40s would also seem to underscore the assumption that politics has done nothing but make life worse for the villagers.)

The remote mountain village setting is also significant. It is called Stunted Flats because the poverty-stricken inhabitants all suffer from Kashin-Beck disease, a degenerative bone disease that leaves them stunted, deformed, and crippled. On a symbolic level, of course, the political movement as it unfolds in the village represents the Cultural Revolution in microcosm and the residents represent China's masses, crippled and deformed by nature and the political system. The villagers live in poverty, struggling for freedom from the realm of necessity. The pursuit of food and sex occupies most of their time. They are largely ineffectual and powerless in dealing with political issues. By contrast, the two representatives of the Communist Party are much freer and not subject to such harsh constraints.

Political control over the village has been exercised by an old-guard revolutionary, Liu Changsheng, also referred to as Director or Commune Head Liu. Over the years since the victory and the establishment of the People's Republic of China in 1949, he has grown complacent. Now comfortable in his position, he enjoys food and drink, as well as the favors of one of the village women, and has no interest in overturning the status quo. He is not a severe master, and basically desires to live and let live.

However, Zhang Weiguo, one of the educated youth who went down to the countryside to transform China, has been living in the village for six years. Known as Kugen'r, or "root of suffering," he is the orphan son of a Party martyr and has chosen to steel and temper himself in the remote country. Vain, conceited, and ambitious to advance himself as a revolutionary, he has not made much headway. His vanity is subtly depicted when he goes to the eye doctor to be fitted for glasses he does not need, because he likes the cosmetic effect. His journal, which is also a fictionalized account of his life and work at the village, portrays himself as a revolutionary hero. Kugen'r, while paying lip service to the goals of the revolution, is in it to advance himself. He has little stomach for Director Liu's way of life and slack principles, and would like nothing better than to put him in his place.

Uncle Gimpy, like most of the villagers, works hard for the basics of life. Despite being called a rich peasant, he has actually spent much of his life caring for the village donkeys. He is well liked by the villagers, but must be trotted out as a class enemy every time the Party orders a political movement to be undertaken. He is subject to not only the laws of the realm of necessity but also the rather arbitrary laws of politics. His decision to end his own life is the only gesture at freedom he can make within a crushing system, and his death is the catalyst that finally precipitates the denouement of the political struggle between Liu and Kugen'r. Just before hanging himself, Uncle Gimpy, in particularly self-ironic form, wonders what the Communists will do after he is gone, since there are no other class enemies in the village.

Nuanyu, the main female character, is not actually from Stunted Flats, and is therefore also healthy and sound in body. In a sense, she represents the healthy and fructifying aspects of nature not subject to deformation by political power. She and her family arrived in Stunted Flats fleeing the famine that resulted from the disastrous Great Leap Forward. Her younger brother dies there, and Nuanyu is married off to one of the village men, or so she thinks. She in fact "weds" the entire village, because the village has provided the goods for the "bride price." After the deaths of her husband and her infant daughter, she enters into a polyandrous relationship with the remaining village males. Cherishing her, the village looks after her; she does light jobs for high work points. It can be argued that Nuanyu and the village men are practicing a form of communism. However, their "primitive" communism is not the ideologically pure variety that the puritanical Kugen'r has strived to inculcate in the villagers for six years. In the poorest parts of Shanxi, such relationships were practiced, though not generally utilized as a topic for literature, until the 1980s and '90s.

Li Rui's revolutionary novel, therefore, stands as an indictment of the period and a critique of the ideological literature of previous decades. The revolution as depicted here has nothing to do with the idealism of proletarian or revolutionary fiction; rather, it is a nexus of conflicts of self-interest conducted under the guise of political and social change. The new society and the revolution are gamed by the self-serving—the complacent and the conceited—for their own ends, which are basically sensual and vain. The revolution is not about uplifting the masses, transforming China or the world, but rather about promoting one political or ideological faction at the expense of all else. On the levels of form and content—the high modernist style and polyandrous relationships in rural Shanxi—the novel stands as a critique of the one-dimensional proletarian fiction that embodied the idealistic metanarrative of the Cultural Revolution and shaped the minds of a generation. *Trees Without Wind* is one of the author's finest novels, and arguably one of the best ever written about China's Cultural Revolution.

JB

Monterey, Vienna, Beijing

ACKNOWLEDGMENTS

THE TRANSLATOR WISHES to acknowledge the assistance and support of David Wang, Li Rui, Jennifer Crewe, Leslie Kriesel, two anonymous readers, and Yingtsih Balcom.

TREES WITHOUT WIND

At Faxing Temple, the Sixth Patriarch Hui Neng pointed to a banner blowing in the wind and, explaining the world to the assembled monks, said, "Neither the wind nor the banner moves; what moves is the benevolent."

The statesman Mao Zedong announced, "Classes struggle; some classes triumph, others are eliminated. Such is history; such is the history of civilization for thousands of years."

Happy or angry, Cao Tianzhu, the production team leader of Stunted Flats Village, always had one thing to say to sum up the world: "Fuck it all to hell."

In the final moment of his life, Uncle Gimpy summed up the world with one word, which was actually the sound made when the stool he had used for so many years tipped over: clunk.

1

He stood stock still below the cliff and watched that distant silhouette. It jolted with each step, growing shorter and shorter, disappearing from sight—first the legs, then the waist, then the torso, until all that remained was a head swaying on the plateau's edge, which, after shifting twice, also vanished, as if it had sunk into a vast, bottomless abyss. Director Liu, he thought, was walking the fifteen *li* down into the valley. Suddenly he felt the urge to cry and cursed himself inwardly. *Damn! What are you crying about? Why are you so weak?* But he was unable to control himself, and tears rolled down his face to the corners of his mouth, salty. He clenched his jaw for all he was worth on that taste of salt in his mouth. He yelled inwardly at the departing figure that had just disappeared from sight. *By doing what you've done, you're departing from the correct stand. I'm here to change the world; my father was a martyr; I am a child of the Party. How can I be the same as you? We can't be mentioned in the same breath. You don't know how I ache in every bone and joint of my body. Do you know how long six years is? I must do this; I will do it! Don't think I won't!*

The sun had long since fallen behind the western mountains. A cold blue shone over the darkening plateau. The mountains, ranged in layers, went on and on under the vast expanse of the sky. In the boundless open space, you could feel the weight of the blue light pressing down. Several crows, returning home to roost, circled above the cliff; their cawing stitched the vastness and the loneliness together with the withered forest atop the cliff. Licking his lips, he thought Director Liu ought to be disgraced. He tightly clutched several pieces of folded paper in his pocket. When Director Liu handed him the papers, he had said in all seriousness, Kugen'r, these are for you. These blank letters of introduction are not to be taken lightly—they represent the Commune Party Committee's trust in you, the power given to you by the Party. You are the orphan son of a martyr, and the Party must rely on people like you to carry on the work. Looking up at Director Liu, he didn't say a word. Director Liu immediately understood what was going through his mind, but he wanted to avoid being too explicit. Director Liu said, Right, you're not called Kugen'r; your name is Zhao Weiguo, Comrade Zhao Weiguo. The great enterprise of purifying class ranks in Stunted Flats Village is entirely up to you. If in the future you need a transfer, just go to the County Party Office and do the paperwork, and these letters will come in handy. If you have any other difficulties, don't hesitate to make them known to the commune. The Commune Party Committee knows that you have applied for Party membership. Work hard and accomplish something during these great storms, and I'll stand as your sponsor for membership! Director Liu spoke unselfishly. When he finished, he laughed and reached out and patted him vigorously on the back. Still he remained silent, just looking at him, but in his heart he thundered, *I don't need you to bolster my morale. It's clear who the class enemies are. When I strike, I'll seize them. I've been here six years. I requested to come here on my own initiative. Are any of you capable of understanding me? I am my father! I came here to change the world for my father. Why must you go sleep in Nuanyu's nest? Nuanyu sleeps with the class enemy, and then you go and sleep with Nuanyu. You, a Party committee head, and the class enemy sleep with the same woman, and you tell me how to struggle? And you offer to sponsor me for Party membership? You're not qualified!*

Director Liu looked him in the eyes, but knew perfectly well that this was one time there would be no beating around the bush, not this time. Director Liu laughed again—the only thing he could do in response was laugh inwardly. Director Liu said, You're still young; you've never been married, so you don't know how miserable it is without a woman. Nuanyu's place is neat and tidy, and she's a good cook. In this poverty-stricken place of ours, when the work of the revolution is accomplished, there'll be nothing left to do, nothing for amusement. When I came to Stunted Flats Village to work in the countryside, I stayed at Nuanyu's. She has a two-room cave—she lives in one room and I stay in the other. Okay, that's the way it is. There's no use staring at me, just do a good job of purifying class ranks. Director Liu finally said what he wanted to say without beating around the bush any longer. After Director Liu said what was on his mind, he swung his hands and left. After taking a few steps, he turned and said, Weiguo, we've only talked about purifying class ranks. The last time I was here I mentioned the woman; do you like her or not? Is it okay? Why don't you say something?

His face suddenly flushed a bright red, and he was immediately filled with anger and embarrassment. He struggled for a moment before he managed to say a few words through his anger and embarrassment. Staring at Director Liu, he said, I'm not marrying—women are all demons! Director Liu just laughed. Look at you, such a child. I was just asking for others. Why so temperamental? If you're not interested, then forget it. It's okay; put your heart and soul into the movement. So saying, Director Liu walked away, swaying as he stepped. He just stood beneath the cliff watching Director Liu depart. The rays of the setting sun shining behind the western mountains were cold, clear, and clean, making the winter plateau look desolate. One could see a hundred *li* through the barren emptiness. Above him, the crows continued to caw sporadically. He didn't look up—there was no need to in order to know that there were seven of them flying around. For the last six years, he had counted them so many times at the entrance to the village. There had been five then; now there were seven, a total of seven. Flying around like that, they seemed to be quite a few at first glance, but there were only seven. But why were there seven and not eight? What about the odd-numbered one? Who would it nest with? Laying eggs and raising young every year, where did they go? Had they all been eaten by snakes? Without a doubt, coiled around a tree there was a big snake—its mouth opened, showing its long tongue—that swallowed each fledgling, one by one, so that the baby birds didn't even have time to cry out. Pitiful. After so many years, only two had survived. The birds didn't know how to fly. Wouldn't it be okay if they could fly far, far away? Goodness, in six years, in six long years, only two had lived. *How can any of you understand how long six years is? How can you understand me? We simply can't be mentioned in the same breath. You know that Nuanyu sleeps with the class enemy, so why do you want to sleep in her cave? You are a leadership cadre. Why do you fail to meet expectations? Why are you so lacking in the correct stand? I don't need your sponsorship to join the Party, nor do I need you to fix me up with a wife. Can you understand me? You have no idea how every bone and joint in my body aches. Don't think I won't do it; I must do it. Even if I don't do it, Zhao Yingjie will not hesitate to see it through to the end.* It was silent all around. Everything seemed frozen in the still of dusk; no one could hear the thundering of Kugen'r's heart in that frozen stillness or see the salty tear streaks on his face.

Taking the small track east that Director Liu had just taken for 15 *li* down to the bottom of the valley, then following a dirt road large enough for a horse cart another 150 *li* to the east, you'd eventually arrive at the county seat, but not without spending the night in some village along the way. The county seat was where he attended primary school and junior high school, and where he became the orphan son of a martyr. Later, it was there that he encountered that writer and decided to write a novel about his father. He wanted to write about his father, and taking his father in the novel as a model, he came to Stunted Flats Village, deep in the Luliang Mountains, to change the world.

2

Looking up, I saw his bulging crotch. It was the director, a national cadre. He can't control himself even for a moment. *If you can't control yourself, then get along. Haven't you worn out Nuanyu's threshold? Haven't you worn out Nuanyu's kang mat? Whenever you come to Stunted Flats, don't you rush straight to Nuanyu's place, and only after you've slept with her can you hold a meeting and get things done? This time, though, you rushed to see me.* Bending over to put down the axe, I saw those cadre shoes and I knew it was him. Who in Stunted Flats wears cadre shoes? They all wear bulky ones. All smiles, I put down the firewood.

I said, Ah, Director Liu, you're here.

He said, Cao Yongfu.

He doesn't call me Gimpy Five. He calls me Cao Yongfu. I knew it was something bad. I said, Come in and have a rest, have a drink of water.

He didn't say he'd have the water or that he wouldn't. He said, Cao Yongfu, I'm here to purify class ranks.

I said, Ah, public business keeps you busy; it's a lot of work. You have to purify.

His crotch was bulging. I heard Director Liu laugh. I looked up and saw a row of teeth, all black from smoking, as if they had been rubbed with black glaze. I knew that when people wanted to purify class ranks, they really meant me. Damn, the ones who ran away are all good; the ones who got caught are all thieves. *If I had run away with my older brother, what class ranks would you have to purify?*

Director Liu said, Ha-ha, Cao Yongfu, if Stunted Flats didn't have a rich peasant like you, there'd be no class struggle and no political movement to engage in. You're very useful.

I said, Ah, ah.

Later, I saw a bottle of liquor in his bag. Nuanyu says that each time he enters her house, he pulls out a bottle of Wucheng sorghum liquor and noisily thumps it down on the *kang* table and says, In this poor place of ours, there's nothing to do, nothing fun to do. Then he stays. Then he drinks. Then he strips off Nuanyu's clothes and throws them on the *kang*. Then he puts Nuanyu astraddle his legs and, face to face, goes at it for all he's worth. Nuanyu says he goes crazy like a horse, till she's dizzy and wants to pass out. Nuanyu says that while he's going at it he asks a question, just one: Who else do you do it with besides me? Who else do you do it with besides me? Who else do you do it with besides me? I'm so dizzy I think I'm going to die. I can't say a word. I didn't like hearing Nuanyu say this. *Fuck, how can you die? That's what you hope for. Every woman in the world hopes for the same damn thing. Nuanyu, Nuanyu, why don't you care if the men of Stunted Flats are sad? People from Stunted Flats are people too.*

Seeing that bottle of liquor, I said, Ah, come in and rest; have a drink of water.

Director Liu didn't say anything. He turned to leave.

I said, Director Liu, I've got some eggs here. Why don't you take them to have with your liquor?

Director Liu said, Okay, after I eat, I have to pass on some documents from the central authorities to all of you. The movement this time really must be carried out in the spirit of these documents. Chairman Mao said a long time ago, "Class struggle must be grasped effectively." This time, Stunted Flats must seize you, a teacher by negative example.

I said, Sure, sure.

Director Liu glowered. What's that, huh? A rich peasant has no place opening his mouth. Take the eggs.

I just smiled. I didn't say that without a rich peasant like me, what ranks would their classes have? What could they purify? *What good would your documents from the central authorities be? All you know is getting over to Nuanyu's as quickly as possible. Do you know for whom Nuanyu pours your liquor? That part of your Wucheng sorghum liquor is poured out for me? Nuanyu pours the liquor for me and says, Uncle Gimpy, you're a good man. You feel for other people. Nuanyu cries as she speaks, speaks as she cries. She cries and makes me feel sorry and angry that I can't put all the good things in the world before her, just to make her smile. Do you understand? You've never ever noticed; you've never ever understood. What are you glaring at? Your crotch protruding, I know what you're in a hurry for. Tianzhu said the ox belongs to the team, the land belongs to the team, and Nuanyu belongs to the team. You come here as a director and use Nuanyu for nothing. Don't you know how shabby that is? We share Nuanyu; we take care of Nuanyu. All the men in Stunted Flats are fine with that. We're totally willing. Who are you, holding the public's iron rice bowl, and coming here to seize someone else's woman? You're the director. Who can get the better of you? You think I want to talk with you? You think you're so big; Kugen'r thinks he's big too. When I talk with you guys, I have to keep my head raised till my neck hurts. What are you guys doing here at Stunted Flats, anyway? Wouldn't the people of Stunted Flats live fine without you? If you guys hadn't showed up, would anyone know of the existence of Stunted Flats? Wouldn't we go on living in peace, the way we'd done for generations? If someone's deformed, what of it? If someone's stunted, what of it? You big guys come and mix everything up in the world till there's not a decent place to live. You guys can't manage your own lives, and you want to screw everyone else's up as well. Are you guys even human? You're worse than oxen in a pen.*

3

Never in my life will I forget the way my second little brother looked when he ate.

My second little brother put down his rice bowl, covered his belly with his hands, and began to cry. His bowl was still half full of noodles. Too much elm bark had been added to the noodles, reddish and wide and flat; you couldn't even tell there was corn meal in them. Covering his stomach, my little brother cried to me, Sister, sister, my stomach hurts; it hurts so bad, sister, it hurts so bad! I turned my head to look at Dad, who had already eaten six bowls. He was standing next to the pot, holding his bowl. Mom had buried her head in her huge coarse bowl and was slurping up her noodles. She had already eaten five bowls. I hadn't had a single bite; I couldn't eat one bite. I was dressed in red, sitting on a bench under the big sun, watching them eat. I wanted to see how much they could eat. I couldn't see anyone's face under the big sun; all I could hear was the slurping. Holding his stomach, my little brother cried to me, Sister, sister, it hurts so bad! It hurts so bad! I'm going to die! Sister! I suddenly stood up, knocking over the stool. Only later did I see that my leg had a bruise the size of an egg where I had bumped it.

Standing up, I shouted, Dad! Dad! You've eaten too much! Why don't you look at little brother—he's going to burst! You just keep eating!

Only then did Dad put down his bowl and turn and say, Huniu'r, Huniu'r, you bastard, you've made me lose face. You little brat, you haven't eaten more than a few bowls. You little motherfucker, can't eat any more, can you? I'm going to beat the fucking hell out of you! Dad swore as he took off his shoe and raised it above his head. See if I don't beat the fucking hell out of you! See if I don't beat the fucking hell out of you!

The slurping in the courtyard suddenly ceased as everyone looked up from their bowl, looking at the shoe my father was holding. I ran to my little brother, whose lips were really blue. I shouted for all I was worth, Dad! Dad! Hurry and help Second Little Brother! He is surely going to die!

Everyone in the courtyard was stunned, dumbfounded; they all sat there holding their huge bowls, mouths hanging open, not saying a thing, not eating noodles. Under the bright and dazzling sun there were only my little brother's blue lips and that half-eaten bowl of red, wide, flat noodles. As my second little brother breathed his last, he said to me, Sister, sister, I'm so hungry, Sister. . . . That was what my second little brother said most often on the road as we fled famine in our old home. All day long, he'd hold onto my lapels, saying, Sister, I'm so hungry. Second Little Brother, Second Little Brother, you lived until you burst. How could you say you were hungry? See, your stomach is as hard as a rock. How could you say you were hungry? Brother, brother, say something, why don't you say something? Dad, Dad, little brother really is dead, he really did burst!

My dad, still holding his shoe, fell to the ground with a thud and began whacking the top of his head for all he was worth, until the yellow earth on the bottom of his shoe covered his head and face. Dad said, Huniu'r, Huniu'r!

The bowl my mom was holding crashed, breaking to pieces, and before standing up, she bent over and puked up all the noodles she had eaten.

At that time, everyone in Stunted Flats had gathered in the courtyard. Only when they had all stood up did I clearly see how short all the deformed people in the village were. Only then did I see what the lips of a person who died from a busted gut looked like. Under the bright and dazzling sun, little brother's lips were blue, so dark as to terrify a person.

After the wedding and burying my little brother, I saw my parents and my other little brothers and sisters out of Stunted Flats. I saw them as far as the bottom of the earthen cliff, where I halted. I said, Dad, Mom, I'll say good-bye here. Don't bother to come and see me later, and don't tell my brothers or sisters to come and see me. And don't send a letter asking about me. I don't want to know anything or see anything. Here is where I am, and I'm not going anywhere else. I'll just stay here and watch over Second Little Brother. I'm afraid Second Little Brother will get lonely here by himself and think of home. Someday, I'll die here and keep him company.

Dad cried. Mom cried. My brothers and sisters all cried with them.

I said, Don't cry. What are you crying for? Don't you have a bag of corn? Second Little Brother died. Didn't they make up for your loss with this young donkey? In principle, he died because he overate; no one had to compensate for anything, but they did, because they're good folks. Who cares if someone is tall or short? Having a good heart is better than anything else. Women are just women. If they go someplace else, they're still married, right? I have no regrets, really, no regrets. I'm just sorry I didn't keep my eye on Second Little Brother and keep him from eating so much; that way he would still be alive. I just regret I didn't keep my eye on him. I didn't know what was going on at the time; my eyes were wide open, but I was like a dummy. I just regret I didn't keep my eye on Second Little Brother. If I had, I wouldn't have let him eat another bowl, no matter what. If he hadn't eaten that last bowl, he'd be on his way home with you right now.

Dad kept crying. Mom kept crying. All my brothers and sisters were crying.

I didn't cry. I couldn't cry. I said, Stop crying, what are you crying for? Even if you keep crying, you still have to leave, right? Hurry up, get along with you. Don't cry. If you don't leave, I'm going back to the village.

Mom sat down on the road of yellow earth; she slapped the yellow earth with the palms of her hands and began to wail.

Mom said, Nuanyu, Nuanyu, Nuanyu.... How's your mom going to go on living? Haven't I harmed you? Huh?

I squatted and held my mom. I said, Mom, you can't say that, we have a family; we're still alive, aren't we?

I couldn't help crying. I'm not made of stone.

Only after I got pregnant did that guy who died young tell me that the bag of corn belonged to the team and the donkey belonged to the team. The grain, food, and oil for the wedding all belonged to the team. I said to him, Tell me, who got married, you or the team? He just held his head in his hands without uttering a word. I said, Aren't you going to say anything? He lowered his elbows and turned and said, Nuanyu, Tianzhu said that everyone has to help out in matters that involve us all. I said, What do you mean, "everyone"? You had damned well better explain it to me. He just cried and said, Nuanyu, Nuanyu, can't you see how pitiful things are for the men of Stunted Flats? All the village men, young or old, are poor bachelors. Didn't your family come here fleeing famine to marry off a daughter? No woman ever comes here to get married. He stood next to the stovetop in the kitchen, his face not much higher than the pot lid. I was frightened by his crying face, and I felt sorry for him. Don't talk to me about being pitiful or not. Tell me clearly what it is that you guys plan to do, you bunch of runts. In a flash I no longer saw his face in the pot lid; I just heard him beneath the stove saying, Nuanyu, Nuanyu, I didn't want to do this, I'm kneeling before you; can't I give back the things owed to the team? Don't be angry. Don't cry. I swear I'll tell Tianzhu that you're not willing and that I'm not willing. I'll return everything to them. If I can't handle this, then let me become an ox or a horse, let me die like a horse, okay?

What sort of oath did he swear, that short-lived guy? He died even before Little Cui was born.

Dad! Mom! Second Little Brother!

Heavens! Heavens! I fuck your ancestors! Heavens!

4

I took her in my arms and gave it to her good. She just shouted. She's a good woman. Nuanyu, Nuanyu, you're a good woman! You wouldn't like it if a living immortal or Heaven replaced her. I gave it to her again; she just shouted, shouted for her dad and shouted for her mom. Shouting and shouting, it scared me. She shouted, Second Little Brother, Second Little Brother! I stopped what I was doing and patted her face. I said, Nuanyu, Nuanyu, Nuanyu, wake up. Why are you shouting for your little brother? Isn't he dead? Her face was covered with tears; my hand was wet wiping them away. She opened her eyes and cursed me, Who told you to stop, damn it? Who told you to stop, damn it? What business is it of yours who I shout for? I'll shout for whoever I want! Little Brother! Little Brother! Little Brother! You hurt Little Cui! She just sobbed. The woman is a demon. You can never figure her temper. At a time like that when she was so happy, she shouted for a bunch of dead people. I held her in my arms. I said, Okay, okay, go ahead and shout, go ahead and shout, shout for whomever you want to shout.

I wonder when the time will be right to tell her. I've been a revolutionary for so many years, and I've never had to do anything to cause such sadness. I've been the head of the commune for more than ten years, and wherever I go I'm in charge of others. How can I let a woman like her control me? How much longer can I keep the words I've had in my heart for two or three years bottled up? According to the present revolutionary situation, what I have to say is a little risky. But I can't very well keep it to myself till the day I meet Marx in Heaven, can I? The revolution does not forbid divorce or forbid marrying, does it? By divorcing and then marrying Nuanyu, I'm still engaged in revolutionary work and not going against principles, right? Besides, the director of the commune is human. I've spent more than ten years in this poor and remote place where no one can make a home, and I've never once said no to the Party. If I said one no to my wife, it would not go against principles. What kind of woman is this? Oh, what a woman!

I took her in my arms and gave it to her again. I asked her, Nuanyu, Nuanyu, who else do you do it with besides me? Panting, she couldn't reply. I asked again, Who else besides me do you do it with? Are you going to tell me or not?

Oh, what a woman! Good Lord!

I wanted to ask her at such a time, because she always tells the truth at times like this. Someday I want to get a straight answer from her. *My whole life, I've diligently and conscientiously engaged in revolutionary work. I've never risked anything. Would I risk everything for a few words of truth, would I?*

She said, I'm tired. She said, I've worked up a sweat and want to get dressed.

I said, Don't, I want to look some more.

She said, Look at what? You've finished and now you won't let me get dressed.

I said, Nuanyu, I want to ask you something.

She said, What do you want to ask? You ask questions all day long.

I said, You must tell me the truth.

Pulling her clothes toward her, she said, I have given myself entirely, what else could be the truth?

I said, You must tell the truth, and I'll tell you something true too. Who else have you slept with besides me?

She looked at me and said, I'm not your wife, and you want to bother with who I sleep with. I sleep with whoever I want.

I said, Of course I want to bother. I want to marry you.

She pulled at her clothes again. You mean as a second wife?

I said, No, I'm not joking. I want to divorce my wife and then marry you.

She said, Have you forgotten your surname?

I said, Liu, my name is Liu Changsheng. Look at you, how can I make you believe me?

She said, Liu Changsheng, you bring the divorce papers here and let me see them, and then I'll believe you.

The sunlight streamed through the hemp-paper window, clearly revealing Nuanyu's body. I removed the clothes she had just thrown over herself. I said, I'm going to push ahead with this regardless and accept any disciplinary action! A person can't spend their whole life in this poor valley and spend their whole life in revolutionary work and not do something for themselves, right? I'm going to push ahead and not be the commune head!

Nuanyu didn't say anything. Nuanyu sat naked on the *kang*, laughing grimly at me.

I said, Don't laugh, I'm going back to the commune and take care of this after I have passed on the central documents.

Nuanyu said, Then I'll wait till the sun rises from behind the western mountains just once.

5

By the time I opened my eyes, Little Cui was dead. I fell asleep when it was nearly light. I had been awake for three days, but when it was nearly light, I couldn't stay awake any longer, so I slept. When I opened my eyes, Little Cui was dead. I pulled open my shirt and put Little Cui to my breast. The child didn't open her mouth, and my milk ran, covering her face. I screamed, Cui'r, Cui'r, Cui'r, Cui'r. . . .

By the time I opened my eyes again, Little Cui's body was already stiff.

I saw my little brother sitting at the end of the *kang*. I said, Little Brother, didn't I tell you that when I died I'd be buried beside you and be your companion? So why are you in such a rush? Little Cui was just a baby, only ten months old. Why are you in such a rush?

My little brother said, Sis, I'm hungry.

I said, I can't do anything about your being hungry. I have to bury Little Cui, I don't have time to cook for you.

My little brother said, Sis, I'm hungry.

I opened my shirt again; my chest was covered with milk. I said, If you're hungry, have some milk.

My little brother pressed close to my breast.

I wept. I said, Little Brother, Little Brother, Little Brother, you killed Little Cui. Why are you in such a rush? Cui'r was only ten months old....

My little brother said, Sis, I'm hungry.

I cried; I said, Little Brother, if you're hungry, eat. When Cui'r is gone, you can look after her; she was only ten months old.

When my little brother departed, I made some clothes for Little Cui. Before the clothes were finished, the village women showed up. The women said, According to the rules here, dead babies are not buried, they must be placed on the wild mountain slopes; if you bury a dead child, it can become a demon and return and take away another child. I put down my needle and thread and picked up the cleaver. I said, Get out of here, you turtle spawn. I'm not from here and I don't care about your damned rules. Clamoring, the women ran out shouting, The woman is crazy! She's going to kill someone!

When the clothes were finished, I dressed up Little Cui as pretty as a flower and buried the little flower next to my little brother. After I buried her, I said, Little Brother, take good care of Cui'r for me. You have to be an uncle to her. I said, Cui'r, keep your uncle company. Let your mom know if you're hungry; I'll squeeze out some milk here. I opened my shirt and squeezed out all of my milk. I said, Cui'r, Cui'r, drink up, Mom has lots of milk.

Every day, I cooked at home; every day, I took food to them. I couldn't let the two kids go hungry.

Uncle Gimpy said I took food for three days. On the third night, holding a bowl, I saw Uncle Gimpy squatting under my window.

I said, Uncle Gimpy, why aren't you at home asleep?

Uncle Gimpy said, Nuanyu, don't take any food to the graves.

I said, Why aren't you at home asleep? Can't you see it's nearly light?

Uncle Gimpy said, Nuanyu, I've been keeping watch here for the last three nights.

I said, Aren't you tired, Uncle Gimpy?

Uncle Gimpy said, Nuanyu, I'm afraid something might happen to you. How can someone eat after they're dead, Nuanyu? Think about it. Little Cui and your little brother are both dead. How can they eat?

Suddenly it was all clear. I sat on the threshold and began to cry.

Uncle Gimpy said, Nuanyu, cry if you feel like it. Have a good cry. Tianzhu and the others are waiting at the graveyard. Everyone's afraid something might happen to you.

When I sat on the threshold, Uncle Gimpy was a head taller than I was. He put his hand on my head and said, Everyone's worried about you; everyone feels so sorry for you.

I pressed against his chest and sobbed.

I said, Uncle Gimpy, Uncle Gimpy, I really want to become deformed, the same as all of you. I'm lonely as hell.

Uncle Gimpy sighed and said, Oh, the deformed are human; those who aren't deformed are also human; human beings have to endure hardship; life is nothing more than two words: enduring hardship. When you think about it, life's pretty meaningless. Cry, cry, cry if you feel like it.

Later, I did what Tianzhu and the others wanted. I said, Tianzhu, don't worry, I'm not going anywhere, I'm not leaving. I'm going to die in Stunted Flats. Even if you don't record high work points for me, don't carry water for me or chop firewood, I promise all of you that I won't leave.

Tainzhu said, That's not right. We have to keep faith and treat people fairly. We all have to take care of you.

I laughed.

Tianzhu also laughed.

Later, I cried.

Tainzhu said, Just look at you, just look at you....

6

I took the steamed cornbread and ran. She shouted Wa-wa-wa, but I didn't pay any attention, I just kept running; after all, she didn't know where I was going.

Going around the pediment, I nearly ran into him. I cursed him, You fucking cunt. You just stand here waiting to run into me. He said, Older Brother, I want to go with you. I said, Go do what? Go where? He said, I saw you take the steamed cornbread, I know where you're going. I hit him with my fist. He started crying. If you don't take me, I'll tell Dad ... if you don't take me, I'll tell Dad.... I said, Second Dog, don't cry. What the hell are you crying about? If you dare tell Dad, I'll slug you! He kept on crying. If you don't take me.... All I could say was, Okay, come with me. When we go through the drainage hole at the foot of the courtyard wall, you have to be quick. If you make a sound, I'll slug you. He laughed and said, Okay, Brother. So off we ran.

Lying on our bellies at the mouth of the drainage hole, I called, Blackie, Blackie. Blackie came out of the cave and I gave him the steamed cornbread and said, Eat, I smeared some sheep fat on it. Blackie ate the cornbread, and the two of us crawled through the drainage hole and quietly pressed against the window. Second Dog tugged at my clothes, saying, Brother, Brother, I can't see a thing. Quickly lowering my head, I clenched my teeth and said, Keep quiet, otherwise they might hear. I'll fucking beat you up. I pressed close to the window again. Everything in front of me was black; I couldn't see a thing either. After a while, I could see. It was the same as last time: they weren't wearing any clothes; they were naked. This one was on top for a while and then that one. As we watched for a while, that's the way it was. I tugged at Second Dog and said, Let's go. Second Dog pouted. I didn't pay any attention to him and made my way out through the drainage hole, with Second Dog following. I knew he didn't have the guts to stay there on his own.

Second Dog sat on the ground muttering, Brother, I didn't see anything.

I said, There wasn't anything good to see, just two people not wearing any clothes, bare-assed naked.

Second Dog said, Was Nuanyu bare-assed too?

I said, Yes.

Second Dog said, So what has she got? I've seen Mom naked.

I said, You're good for nothing, how can she compare with Nuanyu? You're an idiot too.

Blackie came out of the drainage hole and joined us. Blackie sniffed me and then sniffed Second Dog. Then he sat down facing the two of us. I said, You're so fucking dumb, even Blackie is smarter than you. Blackie licked me.

I said, Wait till I grow up. I'm not going to be deformed, I'm going to be as tall as Kugen'r, and I'll marry Nuanyu.

Second Dog said, I'm not going to be deformed either. I'm going to marry Nuanyu too.

I said, You're really dumb. If I marry Nuanyu, you can't. Get it?

Second Dog said, Why not? Dad said Nuanyu is the team's Nuanyu, not one person's; you can't marry her, no one can.

I hit him with my fist. I said, I'm going to slug you, you idiot! I'm never going to bring you here again.

Second Dog started bawling, Wa-wa-wa. He cried the same as her—Wa-wa-wa—it was real ugly.

7

I finally pulled some clothes over me, and then he reached out and grabbed my tits. I pushed him away and said, You haven't had enough, have you? What do you take me for? Some animal in a pen? You want me to cook for you without any clothes on? You're not cold, but I am. He just laughed brazenly, Ha-ha-ha.

Kugen'r is the only good person I've met in my entire life; he's the only one who doesn't think about himself. If he doesn't spend all day thinking about those ideas, then he's thinking about other people. I don't say he's good because he doesn't come here, but if I had to marry, I'd marry Kugen'r. Kugen'r's not bad looking and he's not deformed. What's more, he's honest—it would be hard to find another man so honest. Unfortunately, Kugen'r has never so much as smiled at me. *Ha-ha-ha, what are you laughing about?*

I just said to him, Are you going to get dressed? Do you think you look like a commune head, naked like that?

He kept on laughing, Ha-ha-ha, what kind of a commune head do I make here? Here I'm just Liu Changsheng.

I said, And Liu Changsheng knows no shame. Hurry up and put on some clothes. If you can, why don't you hold the meeting naked?

He just kept laughing brazenly, Ha-ha-ha, but finally he stopped. He said, You don't talk nicely. I can't pass on the central documents naked.

Kugen'r once made a fool of me. He hadn't been in the village more than a few days when he came here. He came in with a straight face and said, Comrade Qin Nuanyu. I was confused. Who was he talking to? I just laughed, laughed till I couldn't catch my breath. I said, You're the only one who ever calls me Comrade. Can't you just call me Nuanyu? Kugen'r said, Comrade Qin Nuanyu, I want to talk with you. I said, Don't bother me. If you have something to say, just say it. Kugen'r said, Comrade Qin Nuanyu, as a female comrade, you must pay attention to your influence. I said, What influence? Kugen'r said, You should pay attention to your relationship with several men in the commune. You're a bad influence the way you behave; you do not fit the true color of poor and lower-middle peasants. I pulled a long face. I said, Kugen'r, I don't know what influence is or if the true color you talk about is red or green. All I know is that my whole family lived on the verge of starvation and the people of Stunted Flats saved them. Kugen'r said, Being a female comrade, you must pay attention to your influence—it's an issue of lifestyle.

I just pulled open my clothes and shoved my tits in his face. I said, Don't say such impractical things to me. Are you trying to tell me you've never wanted to take advantage of me? Don't you think I know what it is you dirty men have on your minds? Come here! Aren't you hankering to take advantage of your auntie? I never imagined that Kugen'r's face would blush such a vivid shade of red. Kugen'r suddenly covered his eyes with his hands and shouted, You . . . you . . . as he ran off. I just sat on the threshold and laughed until I cried. I said, Showing you the true color of a female comrade really frightened you. . . . I have some more true color that I haven't shown you yet . . . it would scare you to death. . . . Since then, Kugen'r blushes every time he sees me. When he blushes, I laugh. I love to see him blush.

I said, When will you learn shyness? When will you learn to blush?

He didn't understand, he just kept on laughing, Ha-ha-ha. He said, What would a big guy like me blush for?

I said, I never expected to meet a man who blushes in my lifetime.

He still didn't understand. He said, It won't be easy to show you a red face. I'll drink two *liang.*

I couldn't help it and began to cry.

He said, Look at you, look at you. Okay, I've made you cry again.

I didn't pay attention to him and went on crying.

Later, I stopped crying. I put on my clothes, washed my hands, and cooked him something to eat.

He picked up the warm wine pot and drank three cups straight. His face was so red for a while that it looked like he was bleeding.

He said, How's this, is it red?

I said, Red.

What else could I say besides red? I'm no mute.

8

I think . . . forget it . . . I'm not going to bother telling them; I'll just keep it to myself.

Standing on the stone step, I dumped the straw in the manger. Several donkeys thrust their mouths in together. I scolded them: Hey! You're all like a bunch of kids. I say eat and you're all in a rush, can't you modestly decline? Don't you know any shame? Let me see, who's still pushing? Who's still pushing? Hearing me scold them, they felt ashamed; they stretched their necks and backed away from the manger, looking at me with their big moist eyes. I went soft. I encouraged them, I didn't say don't eat; the feed hasn't been mixed yet, has it? I still have to add the bran and the soybean cakes. What's so good about straw all by itself?

I hurried and added the bran and soybean cakes, sprinkled in two ladles of water, and stirred it together, letting the water soak in, the aroma of the bran and soybean cakes spread. I patted the remnants from my hands and said, Okay, eat, hurry and eat. Once again they thrust their mouths into the manger and began eating, *crunch, crunch, crunch*. Taste good? I asked. They flicked their ears in response. I leaned against the manger, watching them eat. I love to listen to them chewing, *crunch, crunch, crunch*, more than listening to opera. Eat, eat up. Erhei butted Dahei with his head; I quickly reached in to block Dahei. I said, Okay, okay, brothers shouldn't fight. You're the oldest, so you have to give way. I scolded Erhei: Erhei, Erhei, behave. If you cause any more trouble, I won't let you eat. Do you see how well behaved Heini and Laoni are? You have no sense of shame. I stroked Erhei's head as I scolded him, and he thrust his head into my bosom. Erhei is very clever, but he knows whose favorite he is. But there is not a mom or dad under Heaven who doesn't favor their own.

I lowered the door curtain, placed the lantern on the windowsill, sat on the bench, and watched the family eat. I'm always saying to Tianzhu that there are not nine households in Stunted Flats but ten. Whatever you say, you've got to add mine. Tianzhu just laughed and said I really need a wife. Tianzhu said, That's fine, Uncle Gimpy, we'll send a palanquin around another day and carry Heini to your *kang* so you two can get married. I too laughed. I said, We can get married—Heini isn't bad looking. Tianzhu said, Bad looking? What are you talking about—look at those ears, look at that face, so slender and pretty! We both laughed, laughed until our tears flowed.

Sitting there, I could see the kitchen fire at the head of the *kang*. The flames were burning and the black beans cooking in the pot were nearly done. I could smell the aroma from there. The lantern shone bright and within its circumference of light, it felt warm. They were enjoying their food. *Oh, happiness in this life is having someone love you.* I wondered if they understood how fortunate they were. *I wish I could grow another pair of legs and stand with them in front of the manger. That would be so nice, having food, a place to live, and someone who loves you. There'd be no need to pass on documents or worry about purifying class ranks.*

I'm thinking . . . forget it . . . I'm not going to bother telling them; I'll just keep it to myself.

She lifted the door curtain, came in, and rushed toward me with her hand extended, shouting, Wa-wa-wa.

I said, You are more on time than a farm animal. How would you like a fried soybean cake?

She was still holding out her hand going, Wa-wa-wa.

I went inside and grabbed a handful and shoved it into her palm. I said, Eat up, you. Oh, I feed you every day, I feed you every day, and now you come back for more. Doesn't Tianzhu ever feed you?

She opened her mouth and was all smiles, *crunch, crunch, crunch.*

I threw open the door curtain and said, Hurry home, you mustn't worry Tianzhu.

She was still smiling and chewing. As she left, she shouted, Wa-wa-wa.

The sky was all black. It was so dark you couldn't see a thing. You couldn't see the mountains in front of you; you couldn't see the trees, or the houses. All you could hear was Wa-wa-wa coming out of the darkness.

Wa-wa-wa!

What is enjoying happiness? What is enduring suffering? Not knowing anything is great happiness; the more one understands, the

more one suffers; the greater the understanding, the greater the suf-
fering. Erhei, what I'm saying is right, isn't it? Forget it . . . there's
no point in telling you. I'll just keep it to myself.

The sky was really black; it was so dark you couldn't see a thing. I couldn't see a thing. It was the same as closing your eyes, wasn't it?

9

When I lifted the lid off the pot, a burst of steam extinguished the oil lamp on the stove. The cave was so dark that nothing could be seen. Third Dog cried, Wa-wa-wa, and she shouted, Wa-wa-wa. Holding the lid, I couldn't move; all I could do was shout, Big Dog, Big Dog, hurry up and find the damned matches and light the lamp. You're as fucking dumb as your mother. Big Dog muttered in the darkness, I found them, stop crying, Third Dog, okay? Big Dog lit the lamp, but she kept crying, Wa-wa-wa. I put down the lid and took off the steamer baskets of cornbread. I pushed her aside. You're always in such a rush, you are; don't you see the little ones haven't eaten? Don't you see I haven't eaten yet, either? After eating, I have to go to a meeting. Why are you in such a rush? Sit down!

I took some steamed cornbread for the little ones, ladled out the thin rice gruel, and placed the pickled vegetables on the table on the *kang*. I said, Big Dog, call Second Dog, Third Dog, and Fourth Dog to come and eat. I placed another portion on the stovetop and said, Okay, stop that caterwauling and eat! If I didn't have these four sons, I'd have fucking got rid of you a long time ago.

By the time I had my bowl in my hands and saw the family by the light of the lamp, I felt disheartened. *I'd be better off joining the oxen in the pen to eat. Fuck it all to hell.*

This afternoon I went to Nuanyu's place and the courtyard gate was shut tight in the middle of the day. *The bastard has time for a break, so he comes up here and keeps you busy.* Big Dog, hurry up, Fourth Dog spilled his rice gruel. You're his eldest brother, and all you do is take care of yourself. Can't anyone eat one meal in peace? Third Dog, it's okay, don't cry; if you cry again, I'll beat the fuck out of you.

I soon saw Uncle Gimpy. The door was open and he came in without making a sound.

I said, Uncle Gimpy, have you eaten?

He said, Yes.

The tobacco basket is on the *kang*, help yourself. I continued eating thin rice gruel; he said nothing but smoked pipe after pipe of tobacco. I could see that he had something on his mind. I said, What is it, Uncle Gimpy?

He said, Commune Head Liu is here.

I said, I know, this afternoon I finally got him to open the door at Nuanyu's place.

He said, Tianzhu, he's here to purify class ranks, for class rectification, but it's actually about me. They want to bring up that business of mine again. Tianzhu, can you go after someone else this time? You can't go after me every time.

I put down my bowl of thin rice gruel and said, Uncle Gimpy, this matter is really troublesome; I don't have a say in it. Besides, here in our Stunted Flats, you're the only one with a high enough class status, and then there's Kugen'r, that weak, incompetent baby, who, from morning till night, has to struggle against this and criticize that to score points for himself. At Stunted Flats, we haven't had a day of peace since he arrived—if it's not repairing ditches, then it's building some stockade or the scientific raising of pigs or class struggle, and on top of everything else, I stay up all night writing volumes by the light of a lamp. That weak and incompetent guy won't be satisfied unless he scores points for himself.

Uncle Gimpy asked, Does he score points by purifying my class rank?

Taking a bite of cornbread, I said, That's hard to say; anyway, he wants to score points.

Uncle Gimpy said, All that land is my brother's, not mine. I just look after it for him.

I said, Uncle Gimpy, if I were you, I damned well would have left during land reform.

Uncle Gimpy didn't say anything, but smoked one pipe of tobacco after another. After smoking for a while, Uncle Gimpy said, Purify the class ranks, then purify the class ranks. If the state wants to purify things, can the people do anything but listen? Tianzhu, don't worry; I don't hate you, I just wanted to find someone to talk to.

I said, Uncle Gimpy, just stick it out for two days until Commune Head Liu leaves. It'll all blow over by then. Uncle Gimpy nodded and continued smoking in low spirits.

She shouted, Wa-wa-wa. I said, What are you shouting about now? She put down her bowl and ran into the courtyard, where she squatted and peed. After she finished, she didn't pull up her pants but stood up and shouted, Wa-wa-wa. I walked out and smacked her with the palm of my hand. I said, Are you so shame-less? How many times have I whacked you and you still don't remember? I'm going to beat the hell out of you, you shameless thing!

Uncle Gimpy tried to intervene from the cave, Forget it, Tianzhu, she's just a dumb mute. Beating and scolding her won't do any good. Four sons are good enough. Don't beat her.

I pulled up her pants, hauled her back into the cave, and pushed her onto the *kang*. I said, Big Dog, take care of your mom and put your little brothers to bed, I have to go to the meeting. I took the brass gong from the top of the chest and said, Let's go.

Standing in the courtyard, I banged the gong—*guang*! I struck it again—*guang*! The meeting is about to start.

Uncle Gimpy said, That's a pretty old gong. It was used when the Japs were here harassing us. Someone would stand on the mountain opposite, and when they saw the Japanese soldiers coming, they'd bang the gong and everyone would run. In those days you couldn't run and your mom couldn't carry you, so I had to carry you for her.

I banged it forcefully, *Guang*! *guang*!

Uncle Gimpy didn't say anything more and just shuffled off, shuffled off. At a distance, I heard him sigh.

Near and far, I heard the door hinges creaking. High and low, I saw lanterns and hemp stalks being lit and saw them swaying.

Again I forcefully banged the gong—*guang*! *guang*! The meet-ing is about to start!

I looked up. The sky was full of stars, so many of them and so bright!

I seemed to recall having seen this before . . . right! I was pressed against my mom's bosom. I woke up at midnight, covered with dew. When I looked up through the tree branches, I saw the sky, full of stars. My mom covered my mouth with her hand and said, Don't make a sound or the Japs will find us! At that moment, the stars filling the sky fell into my eyes.

10

There was a lot of smoke and a confusion of people, and the lamplight was dim. Commune Director Liu's face was very red. But Kugen'r was very excited. He put on his glasses.

When he was being fitted for glasses, the old man in the shop asked, Are you a student? Are you nearsighted? No, he said. The old man said, You're farsighted, then? No, he said, I just want to wear glasses. The old man laughed and handed him a pair of glasses. The old man said, Try these plain glass spectacles. He said, Okay. He put on the glasses and looked at himself in the mirror. Wow! They had black frames, just like the pair worn by that writer. The old man said, Are you a student taking the university exam? He laughed and said, No, I'm not taking the exam; I'm going down to the countryside, to Stunted Flats Village. The old man said, Where? He said, Stunted Flats Village, the farthest village from the county seat at 165 *li*. In the mirror, the old man's eyes grew as round as green walnuts. He said no more. How could the old man, whose eyes grew as round as green walnuts, understand him? How could he know that when County Party Secretary Chen asked him, that's what he had said. Kugen'r, pointing to a map on the Party secretary's wall, said, I'll go here.

As Kugen'r spoke, he searched out the farthest black dot on the map. He still didn't know it was called Stunted Flats Village, nor did he know that there was Kashin-Beck disease there. Excited, Secretary Chen clasped his hand and said, You're a good youngster, you have ambitions, like the descendant of a revolutionary martyr. Wearing his glasses, he walked around the streets of the county seat with his head held high. Most of the people in the county seat were familiar to him. He was very pleased with his decision to wear glasses when he saw the startled looks on those familiar faces. He felt he was different from ordinary people in every way.

He was very excited every time he saw the document that Chairman Mao himself had commented on. It was simply a miracle that Chairman Mao's directives could travel over countless mountains and rivers to arrive at Stunted Flats. Peeping through his glasses, he personally read out Chairman Mao's words, one by one:

"This is the best written of all the documents of this type that I have read."

Smoke was rising in the cave, and amid the hubbub, Commune Head Liu became impatient. Commune Head Liu said, Shut the hell up, all of you. Are you listening to Chairman Mao's words or your damned selves? There isn't the least bit of political consciousness among you, is there? Do any of you have the slightest damned idea of the importance of the policies of the Party Central Committee? The cave fell silent after his excoriating rebuke. Commune Director Liu said, Okay, everyone, listen up as Comrade Zhao Weiguo continues reading. Kugen'r, please read.

Kugen'r adjusted his glasses; behind the glass lenses, he sneered. Kugen'r felt there was an immense difference between himself and Commune Head Liu, which was that Liu simply did not understand the masses. *The eyes of the masses are as bright as snow. This afternoon you slept with Nuanyu on this* kang, *and when you slept with her you were carrying Central Committee documents. Do you think the masses trust you? What do you think? In the presence of the Central Committee documents, you stripped off Nuanyu's clothes piece by piece until she was naked, then you got undressed yourself. How can the masses be concerned about Party Central Committee policies? The only thing the masses are concerned about right now is the matter of you and Nuanyu. Don't think I don't notice, and don't think you can escape Zhao Yingjie's eyes.*

Commune Head Liu said, Kugen'r, hurry up and read.

". . . we have also organized the masses to study Chairman Mao's theory, guiding principles, method, and policies for carrying out revolution under the dictatorship of the proletariat, and for mass criticism of the plot by the Chinese Khrushchev and his representatives to subvert the dictatorship of the proletariat and the crime of vainly attempting to restore capitalism . . . 'the tree may prefer calm, but the wind will not subside'; class struggle is independent of man's will. . . ."

Do you know who Khrushchev is? What country he is from? Do you know who the Chinese Khrushchev is? Chairman Mao says that we must constantly be vigilant against the Khrushchevs sleeping beside us. Understand? You don't understand a damned thing except that it's your old lady sleeping beside you. Now isn't that the same as the restoration of capitalism? Do you know what "the tree may prefer calm" means? It means the tree wants to stop and rest, but the wind blows and blows, and even if the tree wants to stop, it can't; even if it wants to stand, it can't.

That's the way class struggle is, no one has a choice—you might not want to struggle, but you have to! Understand? All of this is principle. Kugen'r, read.

"Organize the masses to recall past suffering and think over the source of present happiness, eat a poor meal to recall past suffering, perform operas to recall past suffering, sing songs to recall past suffering. . . . Once, when eating a poor meal to recall past suffering, everyone wept as they ate. Some sang 'Forget Not Class Suffering.' At such a time, everyone's criticism of China's Khrushchev grew angrier. In anger they took a group of capitalist roaders to the factory cafeteria to criticize and denounce them."

At Stunted Flats, we must recall past suffering and think over the source of present happiness, and we must recall the sufferings in the old society and think about the present happiness in the new society. Can you all sing songs about past suffering? Never heard one? Let me sing a bit for you: Stars above fill the sky, the crescent moon is bright and shiny; the production team a meeting holds, pouring out grievances, righting wrongs; the evil old society, hatred of blood and tears of the poor; hatred beyond measure, hatred beyond measure fills my heart; bitter tears I cannot hold back, it all fills my heart. Okay, that's enough. You get the idea. Where there are wrongs, there is hatred; where there is hatred, there is drive; only where there is drive can there be firm, accurate, and victorious struggle. Tell me, whom should we struggle against here in Stunted Flats? You don't say anything when asked. Are you all mute? Speak up!

The atmosphere in the cave became more animated. No one knew that Commune Head Liu could sing or that he had such a ringing voice. Tianzhu said, Sing some more, Commune Head

Liu. That was pretty good. If you sing some more for us, I'll sing a passage from the drama *Injustice to Dou E*, which is also pretty bitter and tragic. Nuanyu squeezed through the crowd, poured a bowl of water, and carried it to Commune Head Liu. Nuanyu said, Here, have some water. Commune Head Liu, excited and happy, took the bowl and drained it at one go. Commune Head Liu said, Don't get the idea that I'm drunk. Do you think one bottle is enough for me? One time, at a meeting in the county seat, me and the other commune heads got together to drink, and I downed two fucking bottles by myself. And was I drunk? Not by a damned long shot! Kugen'r, read, continue reading.

"One counterrevolutionary, when working after being made to wear a counterrevolutionary's hat, saw that the militiamen who were overseeing her were not paying much attention, and rushed to the fourth floor of the women's dorm and then hurled herself to her death. Of course, suicides by counterrevolutionaries are unavoidable, but one less teacher by negative example. . . ."

Commune Head Liu saw Uncle Gimpy withdrawn off in a corner. Think, everyone, who is our class enemy in Stunted Flats? Uncle Gimpy kept his head lowered, but he clearly felt all eyes pressing on him.

Kugen'r was agitated. Seeing the stern look on Commune Head Liu's face, Kugen'r thought, *You and the class enemy sleep with the same woman. What is your political stand?* Agitated, Kugen'r suddenly discovered that Nuanyu was staring at him. After arriving in Stunted Flats, Kugen'r quickly realized that Nuanyu was a special woman. Her husband had died, but she and all the poor unmarried men in the village had a secret relationship. Kugen'r had once resolved to stop her, but he immediately found himself embarrassed. Nuanyu didn't take him seriously and had easily defeated him with her two breasts. All of Nuanyu's eccentricities and unrestrained behavior were protected by a strong and secret safety net of the men. The men of Stunted Flats gave her the easiest jobs, but gave her the most work points. The men of Stunted Flats were perfectly happy to support this eccentric and unrestrained woman. Kugen'r couldn't imagine how many men it would take to satisfy her. After so many men, she still maintained her relationship with Commune Head Liu and seemed to particularly like him. After his defeat, Kugen'r had often discovered her burning hot eyes on him. And every time it happened, he would be filled with shame and anger. Those two snow-white breasts burned amid his shame and anger, causing him to blush furiously. When she saw him blush, a smile would appear on Nuanyu's face. The moment she smiled, Kugen'r would feel totally different, as if he had fallen to earth from the sky. Kugen'r hated her, hated that smirk of hers that he couldn't overcome. Kugen'r said, She's a demon! In the village, Nuanyu frequently told of her sufferings, how her brother nearly starved at first and how later he ate himself to death. She told how she, a sixteen-year-old girl, was exchanged for a bag of corn, and how her brother's life was exchanged for a donkey. She usually wept as she spoke. Nuanyu said this was all the result of the Great Leap Forward—there was no way that a single *mu* of land could produce ten thousand *jin* of grain. When Nuanyu talked of such sufferings, she made no distinction between the old society and the new, and she had absolutely no class stand or class sentiment. Chairman Mao said that educating the peasants was a serious issue. Chairman Mao's words were uttered with someone like Nuanyu in mind. How could he not educate such masses? *How can they understand me? They are entirely different. How can they understand me? I am my father. I am here to change the world for my father. There will come a day when I will teach that smirking woman. Zhao Yingjie fears no difficulty, and there's no way he'd fear a smirking woman like you!*

Commune Head Liu suddenly shouted in anger, Damn it, who was snoring? You don't want to listen to documents from the central authorities? You don't want to hear Chairman Mao's directives? You can just die of drowsiness! If anyone snores again, we will not close the meeting tonight. Let's see who dies of drowsiness and who doesn't. Kugen'r, read it to them again, from the beginning.

"This is the best written of all the documents of this type that I have read...."

Smoke, bitter and hot, began once more to rise. Tianzhu slept holding his nose, fearful lest Commune Head Liu hear him snore.

11

Grumbling, they all stared at me. All he has to do is show up and they all stare at me, just wishing they could have me. *Watch, watch as I carry this bowl of water to him. You bunch of weaklings, even bound together you'd not dare raise a finger against him. You don't dare do anything but stare at me. The moment he leaves, you all become heroes. You all curse him, railing with all kinds of dirty language.* Just after he left, Tianzhu brought that braying donkey and hitched it at my door. That fucking Tianzhu said, Hey, Nuanyu, it's here for your pleasure tonight. Its thing is much bigger than Commune Head Liu's. If you don't believe me, just give it a try. I threw a basin of water I'd used to wash the rice over him. Your auntie will sleep with whoever she wants. If any one of you can supply the betrothal gifts, then he can marry me. A whole village of men can't stop one guy, but sure can come here and give me trouble. You're all men; your things are all kneaded by his woman. You guys can go service the sows. Wiping the water from his face, Tianzhu opened his mouth in a toothy smile. Tianzhu said, Okay, woman, why such a bad temper? What about leaving this hired donkey to be at the beck and call of that fool wife of mine? *Men are all good for nothing. I want to see if anyone dares step forward to contradict him. I'll marry the man who does, first thing tomorrow morning. A bunch of good-for-nothings—even in their dreams they dare not say no to him. Just stare with your eyes wide open. I'll marry him just to piss you all off.*

I carried the bowl of water to him and said, Here, have some water.

He started to smile. *What are you smiling at? You can't even keep up appearances. What sort of commune head are you, laughing like that?*

I glanced at them and I said, Hurry and drink up. I'll get you more if you want it.

Every last one of them raised his head. Their eyes were all fixed on the ground. It was the same the day my little brother died—a whole courtyard full of runts with their heads raised, not saying a word; a whole courtyard full of staring eyes.

When he put his face in the bowl, I turned and looked at Kugen'r. He suddenly blushed and I smiled. *I wonder when you'll become a real man.*

When he put down the bowl, Kugen'r's face was no longer red. Kugen'r said, A moment ago, Commune Head Liu called upon everyone to speak. I would like to express my own view. I believe that although our Stunted Flats is a small village, the situation of class struggle is actually extremely complicated. Kugen'r glanced at him and said, Some comrades have departed from the correct stand, confusing the issue of work style and class enemies. Chairman Mao guides us in saying, "We should support whatever the enemy opposes and oppose whatever the enemy supports." But some comrades persist in mixing their support with the enemy. Chairman Mao says, "Who are our enemies? Who are our friends? This is a question of the first importance for the revolution." Saying this, Kugen'r glanced at him again. *Kugen'r spends all day beating around the bush saying things no one understands. Never in his life will Kugen'r guess the issue of Stunted Flats; never in his life will he observe those staring eyes.*

Listening to Kugen'r, he smiled and said, Kugen'r has tempered himself well in the last few years and has finally made progress. That is why the Commune Party Committee has agreed to have Kugen'r assume the position of head of the Stunted Flats Political Team. He smiled again and said, What does the second paragraph on page 3 of the quotations of Chairman Mao say, Kugen'r? "We must have faith in the masses and we must have faith in the Party. These are two cardinal principles. If we doubt these principles, we shall accomplish nothing." Isn't that what it says? Therefore, you must have faith in the Party. If you fail to do so, you "shall accomplish nothing," right?

As he finished speaking, he handed me the bowl and said, Nuanyu, pour a bowl of water for Kugen'r. He can read again after he's had a drink of water.

I took the bowl and looked at Kugen'r, and then I looked at him once more. I saw all the eyes in the cave fixed on the two of them.

I poured the water, but did not give it to Kugen'r or to him. I walked to the corner and offered it, saying, Uncle Gimpy, have some water. Without looking, I knew how wide the eyes of the two of them were. Both of them must have hated me right then. Served them right!

12

How quiet it was. It was so quiet that not the slightest sound was heard, no wind, no clouds—only the sun sizzling on the back of your head. I led the milk goat through the woods and heard nothing save the sun sizzling on the back of my head. No gunfire, no cannons, no crying, no shouting; the Japanese blood-spotted bandage flag was nowhere in sight. But Mom? Dad? Grandpa? Grandma? I was so thirsty, I could have died. I pulled the milk goat toward me and said, Lanzi, don't move. I knelt down and drank her milk. Nuanyu was behind us. I said, Nuanyu, aren't you

41

TREES WITHOUT WIND

thirsty? Won't you have some of Lanzi's milk? Nuanyu said, No, I have too much milk and no place for it. I said, Then I'll drink yours, okay? Nuanyu said, No. Where's Mom? Dad? Grandpa? Grandma? I pulled Lanzi toward me and said, Let's go home, Lanzi. The sun sizzled on the back of my head. The first thing I saw on the threshing ground was Huatou. The lower part of Huatou's body was covered with blood, dyeing the ground red. Huatou cried. I asked her, Huatou, Huatou, where are your legs? Who cut off your legs? Huatou said not a word; Huatou turned her two horns toward me and bleated, Moo-moo. Beneath Huatou the ground was all red. Then I saw the flies. A huge mass of them on the sacred old tree, like a living hemp bag spread there. I walked over and the flies buzzed, taking flight, hitting me in the face. I saw Grandpa; he was covered with blood. Grandpa had no eyes and no tongue; his stomach was slit open; his guts hung to the ground. Grandpa's pipe had been tossed on the ground, its copper stem shining. I ran; I shouted, Mom! Mom! I saw my mom in the courtyard of Ugly Baby's house; I saw my grandma; I saw Ugly Baby's mom and her sister; I saw all the women of the village in the closed courtyard. They were all naked and standing white under the sun. All I heard was the sun sizzling on the back of my head. Lanzi butted me from behind. I said, Nuanyu, there's my mom and grandma. I suddenly heard all the women in the courtyard crying. Mom and Grandma called to me, Tianzhu! Tianzhu! What about your grandpa? The women were all crying, all shouting, It's the end, it's the end. How can we go on after this? It's over, it's the end. . . .

As the women cried, the sun became the moon.

The moon slowly came out of the clouds and said, Don't cry, don't cry, you'll only do yourselves harm.

Ugly Baby's grandpa appeared; Ugly Baby's grandpa walked around the village, my brass gong in his hand. He struck the gong as he walked and he struck the gong as he gave everyone heart. The year the Japanese came was a disaster; my fellow villagers, there's nothing strange about it. Holding the gong, Ugly Baby's grandpa sat on the stone roller, crying. He said, Women, don't think of suicide. If you all kill yourselves, who will have babies for us at Stunted Flats? Who will have babies at Stunted Flats? Women, don't take it so hard, okay?

Pointing at a mound, I said, Nuanyu, look, that's the grave of Ugly Baby's grandpa. Over there are the graves of my grandpa, my grandma, my dad, and my mom. Later my grave will be here too.

' Nuanyu nodded and said, These are the graves of my brother and my Little Cui. When I die, I'll be buried with them.

I pushed open the door and entered Nuanyu's cave; Nuanyu didn't even look up. Nuanyu said, Come here. I said, Okay. Nuanyu said, The guys who come to my place don't have wives; you have a wife, but you still come. Why are you so greedy? I said, Nuanyu, is that wife of mine a wife? Is she even human? Nuanyu said, Yes or no, you married her, so who's to blame? I climbed up on Nuanyu's *kang* and took off my clothes. Nuanyu's *kang* was really warm; Nuanyu's body was really soft, so comfortable you'd like to fuck it all to hell forever.

I said, Nuanyu, marry me.

Nuanyu said, No. You have a fool wife at home and you want to marry again? You're dreaming.

I said, I really regret it.

Nuanyu said, Regret what?

I said, That you're not my wife.

Nuanyu said, You're dreaming!

I said, Dreaming? Wish I were, so that I might be satisfied. Fuck it all to hell.

Lanzi butted me from behind again. I pushed her away and said, Lanzi, why do you keep butting me, it hurts!

Commune Head Liu swore at me, Tianzhu, Tianzhu, what kind of damned production team leader are you? The caves are all about to fucking collapse! How much more do you want to sleep? How damned low can your political consciousness be?

Everybody laughed at me. What the fuck are you dreaming about, snoring so loudly? Are you dreaming about taking another wife?

I just smiled. I was just discussing marriage with Nuanyu. If you'd woken me later, there might have been a baby.

Nuanyu swore. Everyone laughed.

I said, Uncle Gimpy, the year my grandpa died by a Jap sword, was that the third day of the seventh month of the lunar calendar?

Uncle Gimpy nodded and said, Yes, that was the third day of the seventh month.

I said, My mom said I was seven years old that year.

Uncle Gimpy said, Yeah, seven years old. That day, your grandpa looked all over the village for you but couldn't find you. No one knew you had taken the goat up to the mountain slope. Your grandpa hadn't been dead more than a couple of weeks when the Japs arrived again. You couldn't run, so I carried you on my back for your mom....

Commune Head Liu said, Cao Yongfu!

Uncle Gimpy looked at Commune Head Liu but said nothing. I knew that Uncle Gimpy was afraid.

13

The steam from that bowl of water rose to strike my face. I rubbed my hands on my pants. I looked up.

I said, Nuanyu...

Nuanyu said, Take the bowl.

I said, Nuanyu . . . Commune Head Liu told you to pour a bowl for Kugen'r.

Nuanyu said, I heard him. This is my house, and I'll pour a bowl for whomever I want. If Kugen'r wants a drink, he can pour it himself.

Beyond Nuanyu, I could imagine how many people were staring at this terrible bowl of water. I said, Nuanyu, Commune Head Liu told you to pour a bowl for Kugen'r.

She suddenly thrust the bowl to my mouth; the hot steam from the bowl assailed my face.

Nuanyu said, Drink up.

I drank. The water ran from my face into the bowl.

When I finished drinking, I stood up at once, went over to the stove, and quickly poured a bowl of water and carried it over to Kugen'r. I said, Kugen'r, have some water; Commune Head Liu ordered that you be given some water.

Kugen'r did not take the water. He said, I don't want any, and I didn't ask you to pour any for me.

Holding the bowl, I smiled at Kugen'r and chuckled, He-he, he-he....

I handed the bowl of water to Commune Head Liu and said, Well then, Commune Head, won't you have a drink?

Commune Head Liu said, Cao Yongfu, how can I drink water you pour?

I stood like a beggar amid the crowd, holding that bowl of water. I chuckled, He-he, he-he....

No one paid any attention to me. I again chuckled, He-he, he-he.

Beneath the oil lamp, I faced so many expressionless faces. Behind each face was a long black shadow. I wondered where I was.

Beneath the oil lamp, my brother said, Little Brother, it's decided, you stay here and look after the land. I said, Older Brother, when will you, my sister-in-law, and the kids come back? My brother said, Don't worry about when we'll be back; someone has to look after the Cao family land. It is the Cao family roots, and people can't leave and take their roots with them. Those who pull up their roots and leave become rootless ghosts. I nodded and said, Older Brother, I'll look after our roots, but come back soon. My older brother nodded but said nothing. My sister-in-law didn't say anything either, but her face was covered with tears. My sister-in-law said, Kids, come here and kneel before your uncle....

Beneath the oil lamp, I faced so many expressionless faces. Behind each face was a long black shadow. I wondered where I was.

My sister-in-law said, Kids, come and kneel before your uncle.... Beneath the oil lamp, I was encircled by the faces of the children looking at me. I cleared my throat, Ahem, stood up. What's this all about? What's this for? Ahem. Tears rolled down my face.

Beneath the oil lamp, I faced so many expressionless faces. Behind each face was a long black shadow. I wondered where I was.

I stood amid the crowd, holding that bowl of water. No one paid any attention to me. I looked like a beggar.

I chuckled, He-he. . . .

14

I was awakened by the cold. I reached out and felt a wet patch in the bedding. I threw off the blanket, sat up, and pushed her away. How could you wet the *kang* again? How can I sleep when it's so wet? Do you motherfucking have to wet the *kang*? See if Dad doesn't beat you when he gets home.

She just cried, Wa-wa-wa.

I quickly shook Second Dog, Third Dog, and Fourth Dog. Hurry and get up. Move over, don't sleep in her piss! Hurry up!

I lit the lamp and jumped down off the *kang*, and from the stove at the head of the *kang* took several handfuls of ash and threw it over the place where she had pissed. I shivered when I crawled back under the covers.

Wait till I grow up and spend my life as an unmarried man. I'll never take a motherfucking idiot for a wife! Not for my whole life!

15

That woman! She carried a bowl of water to me in those soft, slender hands of hers. *She knew you wanted a drink, she knew you wanted a drink, she loves you. That woman!*

She put the bowl of water to my lips and said, Here, have some water.

I smiled; I took the bowl of water. Only when she pressed her thigh against me as I sat on the *kang* did all the men in the room stare wide-eyed. *That woman! You can't guess what she's going to do.* As I was drinking, she said, I'll get you more if you want it. I smiled again. This bastard place is so poor there's nothing here . . . except Nuanyu. Political Commissar Wang of the county military regiment asked me, how old are you, little devil? I said, Thirteen. Political Commissar Wang said, Little devil, when the revolution is victorious, will you be willing to remain here and work? I said, Yes. Political Commissar Wang's home is in the south; you came to this poor place for the revolution. I'm from here, so why wouldn't I be willing? Political Commissar Wang smiled and praised me, Good, that's a good way of putting it. Later, Political Commissar Wang died a martyr's death. After he had sacrificed himself, we, the soldiers of the county regiment, stood around his grave, raised our fists, and vowed we would avenge him and would see the revolution through to the end. As I was swearing my oath with my fist raised, I never really thought I'd one day become the commune head here and spend my whole life in this valley, or that I would meet this woman by the name of Nuanyu. *Ancestors, this leg of hers will be the death of me!*

Kugen'r is such a child. Reading the quotations of Chairman Mao to me. At the age of thirteen I served as Political Commissar Wang's bodyguard; when I was fighting for the revolution, bullets were flying. *And you want to talk to me about political stand? What political stand? In the Yellow Earth Valley Commune, the Party is me and I am the Party and wherever I stand, that is the revolutionary stand. You can't even understand that fucking little point, and you want to talk to me about political stand? Fool!* In another way of speaking, Liu Bei said to Guan Yu that brothers are like hands and feet and that a wife is like clothes; if you lose your hands and feet you're finished, but if your clothes are ruined, you can replace them. *You're such a child—you've never known the pleasures of a wife, do you know how hard it is without a wife? What do you know of a thigh like that? I sleep with Nuanyu because I want to marry her. Do you understand that? The revolutionary committee has only been around for two years and you want to overthrow things, do you? By overthrowing everything, won't that make Political Commissar Wang's death meaningless? This is not the time for overthrowing things; now is the time for purification! Do you understand? PURIFICATION!*

The leg pressed against me is so soft. The only thing I have to figure out right now is who else Nuanyu has slept with. I've spent my whole life in the revolution, and I'd risk it all for the truth. Her legs are so long. After the meeting ends, I'm going to ask her again who she has slept with. Chairman Mao says, "What really counts in the world is conscientiousness, and the Communist Party is most particular about being conscientious." Can this damned matter not be taken seriously? You'll have to come clean and tell me who you've slept with. Who? If there weren't so many people watching, I'd damn well pinch your leg. I'd climb a mountain of swords for that leg, or plunge into a sea of flames. No one had better think of trying to stop me.

After drinking the water, I handed the bowl back to her and said, Nuanyu, pour a bowl of water for Kugen'r. He can read again after he has a drink of water.

After taking the bowl, she threw me a smile. She didn't give the bowl to Kugen'r, she carried it over to Uncle Gimpy, her eyes wide open. That woman fucking cares nothing for class stand. In ten thousand lifetimes you'll never be able to guess what she is fucking going to do. Old Gimpy, Old Gimpy, you really understand nothing; you really have the guts of a leopard; if there is anything to that, you're dead.

Holding the bowl, he stood in front of me, nodding and bowing.

I said, Cao Yongfu, how can I drink water you pour?

Kugen'r and Nuayu heard what I said.

I said, Cao Yongfu, how can I drink water you pour?

Stand? Do you know what my stand was when Political Commissar Wang died the death of a martyr? When Political Commissar Wang fell, his chest was covered with blood. I held him and wept. I said, Political Commissar Wang, Political Commissar Wang, you can't die. . . . Political Commissar Wang opened his eyes and looked at me, smiled, and said, Little devil . . . Political Commissar Wang is finished. I said, Political Commissar Wang, I'll spend my life watching over you, I'll stay right here. *Can you find this stand by reading the quotations of Chairman Mao? I've spent half my life here working and never once said no to the Party. Can you find this stand by reading the quotations of Chairman Mao? There's no need for you to smile—tonight I'm going to give that leg of yours a good pinching.*

16

Kugen'r placed the coal oil lamp on the table in front of the window and turned up the flame. A brilliant golden light seemed to rise from his hands, shining on his thin, determined face. On the wall right next to the table was a portrait of Chairman Mao wearing a cap with a red star on it; it was Kugen'r's favorite picture of Chairman Mao because he too had a thin, determined face, in which you could even detect a trace of sadness. Right next to the portrait were a map of China and a map of the world; on the wall across from the maps was a red poster with yellow letters, a quotation from Chairman Mao that read, "We Communists are like seeds and the people are like the soil. Wherever we go, we must unite with the people, take root and blossom among them." All Kugen'r needed to do was look up and his eyes could take in China and the world, and from his narrow, dark little cave he could enlarge his ideals into a magnificent picture scroll. Kugun'r had intentionally chosen this cave, the highest in the whole village and the remotest, because he knew that whenever the lamp shone in his window, the people could look up at the highest spot and see light. There was a thin, determined face in the light, on which there was a trace of sadness born of ideals. For six years, this window had greeted the sun first every day and been the very last to see off the evening clouds. In six years, or two thousand one hundred days, Kugen'r's ideals had been enriched on a daily basis. With increasing age and maturity, Kugen'r sometimes rejoiced in being the orphan of a martyr. An orphan is a person with no ties, a person with the fewest selfish ideas and personal considerations, a person who naturally exists wholeheartedly for his ideals. The twin joys of having chosen ideals and having been chosen by ideals often stirred up a sense of excitement and pride deep in Kugen'r's heart, which was difficult to express. Kugen'r longed to be tested by all sorts of sufferings on account of this excitement and pride. Deep in the still of night, living alone in the seclusion of his earthen cave, Kugen'r often sank into a profound happiness. On the vast wasteland in the endless night appeared a window like a point of starlight, the light of Kugen'r's spiritual happiness.

He became a martyr's orphan at the age of six. In the summer of his sixth year, he saw his mother, who worked as a cleaner in a long-distance bus terminal, cry. As she wept, she clutched a letter and said, Kugen'r, Kugen'r, your lot is a hard one. At the time he didn't know what a hard lot was. All he knew was that his father, who had gone to Korea as a volunteer soldier, had himself been killed by the American devils, and he had become a child without a father. A year later, his mother bought him a new book bag. She said, You should go to school. Choose a study name and don't call yourself Kugen'r; your father's surname is Zhao, the first in the list of one hundred surnames. Call yourself Zhao Weiguo. Her tears welled up as she spoke, and then suddenly she was lost in thought. When this happened she heard no one and didn't speak, she was so blank she resembled a wooden stool. Later, when he entered junior high school—it was also during the summer—his mom went to work and never came back. The adults told him that his mom had been run over by a bus. She had been sweeping the lot when suddenly she just stood there without moving and a bus came along and ran her down. The adults dressed him all in white and led him behind a coffin to the graveyard. They also told him to kneel at the new grave and kowtow several times. The adults said, Cry, cry, cry. He didn't cry. The whole time, he felt his mind was in chaos. After everything was taken care of and the adults had all left, only then, as he lay in bed, did he realize that he was completely alone. Kugen'r was not accustomed to being alone. When he crouched to drink from the cistern, he saw his face. Like a bolt of lightning, something of great importance came to him. He thought, *My mom didn't die. They never opened the coffin or asked me to look inside. It was empty. My mom didn't die, she never died. And they wanted me to cry. I didn't cry.* With such thoughts, the face of the thirteen-year-old boy reflected in the water was shattered and made hideous by his falling tears. Later the school principal and his teacher said, Zhao Weigou, it would be best if you went to an orphanage. He said, I'm not going. From his book bag he took out a bereaved family pension card and he said, I get twenty *yuan* every month. I have money; I'm not going to an orphanage—I'm a student. My mom taught me how to cook and wash clothes. Besides, no one opened the coffin to let me see if my mother was inside. As Kugen'r spoke, his expression was firm and harsh. His firmness and harshness left the principal and the teacher confused. The principal kept saying, Okay, okay, that's fine. Kugen'r grew even firmer and harsher as he said, I don't care if it's okay or not, I'm not going to an orphanage—I'm a student. The principal said, That's fine, then you can live on campus. The principal also said, Zhao Weiguo, you must keep in mind that it is the Party and the country that are raising you. In the future you must listen to the Party. Kugen'r said, Of course I will. My father was a martyr. My mom said my dad was in a car when the American devils in their planes dropped a bomb, killing him. My father was a martyr. My father died, so I'm now the son of the Party. Of course I will listen to the Party—the Party is my father. The principal and the teacher listened, their mouths hanging open. The principal and the teacher felt that having such a student would constitute a paramount glory.

Over the years, his classmates retained the memory of the scene of his father charging bravely ahead, risking the enemy's fire. After watching the movie *Battle for Triangle Hill*, he could more clearly and concretely hear the sound of enemy aircraft and the exploding bombs. The scream of shells slicing through the air kept him excited, and agitated. This agitation became the inspiration for a novel one summer afternoon. That hot afternoon, to the noisy cries of the cicadas, Kugen'r finished reading the novel *Great Changes in a Mountain Village*. Opening the book, he saw a photo of the author wearing black-framed glasses; inside, the book said it was the story of a demobilized soldier who returns to his poor hometown to change the world. Kugen'r closed the book amid the noisy *chirr* of the cicadas, deciding that he too wanted to write a novel. He wanted to bring his father to life; he decided he wanted to live with his father in this world. This irresistible idea took root in Kugen'r's mind, blossomed, and flourished like a brilliant sunflower. Kugen'r thought, *I am the son of the Party, I am my father.*

Kugen'r placed a thick pile of notebooks in front of him. He was amazed as he weighed his life and his father's life—over two thousand days had been arrested in the thick notebooks, in small, tightly packed words. Even now, some of his early decisions still amazed him; from the very day he arrived in Stunted Flats, he had decided to make his novel and his diary one and the same. On the cover of each notebook, he had written the eye-catching title "A Record of the Stormy Situation in a Mountain Village." The main character in these notebooks wasn't Zhao Weiguo or his father, but a heroic demobilized volunteer soldier by the name of Zhao Yingjie. In six years there wasn't a day that Kugen'r failed to write in his diary; he had his imaginary father pour out his feelings and experiences each day in his diary. Kugen'r would often pause as he wrote, when overcome by tears of emotion. Gradually, as Kugen'r read over what he had written, he was amazed to discover that he was linked in flesh and blood to a common fate with his father, and that they existed as one in the character with the resounding name of Zhao Yingjie.

Kugen'r took his notebook and in it solemnly wrote:

November 5, 1969
Would he actually do it or not? In six years, it was the first time he had encountered such an intense and unavoidable test. He had to courageously decide in line with the position of the revolutionary cause. In the midst of this critical and complicated class struggle, at this critical moment, loyalty to the Party came above all else. Zhao Yingjie had to make his own decision. The highest directive was his beacon light. . . .

17

I was standing in the shadow of the pediment, disinclined to move, listening to everyone as they dispersed, walking away, listening to people open and close their doors. Then nothing was heard and nothing was seen. *Tell me, if they all went off to sleep and didn't wake up and the sun didn't rise, what sort of world would it be? Probably just like this one. Dark, utterly dark, so black you can't see the outline of anything, really dark, the only thing in front of you is blackness that can't be moved or dispersed.*

I didn't take the lantern, I left it at home; I didn't want to leave them in a dark house. I didn't want them to wake up and be confronted by the utter darkness and have them feel afraid. Also, if they woke up with a start—they are not very brave—I didn't want them to be frightened. I'm used to walking at night, feeling my way along in the dark; I've been walking in this little village for forty-five years and couldn't get lost even with my eyes closed. Life is like walking at night, one step at a time—it's all dark with your eyes open, and it's all dark with your eyes closed. You can't move it or disperse it; there's nothing you can do—it's all dark in front of you and all dark behind you. From the very first, in your mother's belly, it's dark; no sooner than you die and your eyes close than you're buried in the ground, and it's dark. They say your soul remains after you die, but who knows if souls come out at night or during the day? If they do come out at night, can they walk in the dark? It's really dark, and it can't be moved or dispersed.

She scared me. She said, Uncle Gimpy.

My heart pounded. I said, Who's that?

She said, Uncle Gimpy, I've been watching you. You're not going home, you're just standing there. What are you doing? What are you doing?

I said, Oh, my good woman. Why don't you hurry home? Are you trying to get me killed? If Commune Head Liu sees, I'll be dead for sure.

She said, He wouldn't dare. I wasn't sold to him. I can talk with whomever I want. If he wants to interfere, he can just stop coming to my place; he can go wherever he likes.

I said, I have to go home and feed them their evening fodder. Get along. You best get going.

I left.

She said, Uncle Gimpy, is anything the matter? I've been watching you here for ages.

I ignored her and kept walking. It was really dark—you couldn't move it or disperse it. A high step, a low step, it was all dark. In the darkness that was as black as lacquer, she kept asking from behind, Is anything the matter? It was really dark—you couldn't move or disperse it.

Finally, I got home. Hearing the door open, Erhei's ears twitched. The warm air hit me. I said, Erhei, I woke you. Erhei flicked his ears. I said, Erhei, it's just as well that you're awake—I'm here to give you a little nighttime fodder. On such a cold night you have to eat your fill; otherwise, how can you keep the cold away? They were all awake. They all squeezed together at the manger. I stirred the feed and they chewed noisily, savoring. *It's my good fortune to spend my life with them. See, they listen to me; they are enjoying their food.*

She nearly scared me to death. She called from outside my door, Uncle Gimpy, Uncle Gimpy, is anything the matter?

I broke out in a cold sweat. I said, What's the matter with you today? Do you have to let him see? What could be the matter? Hurry up, you should leave.

She said, Uncle Gimpy, what are you afraid of?

I said, Hurry up and get along. I'm begging you, okay?

Just as I was speaking, she lifted the door curtain and came in, took a bottle of liquor from her breast, and handed it to me. She said, Here. She said, I don't like seeing you frightened this way. You are a man. Dropping the curtain, she left. Couldn't move it or disperse it; it was so dark you couldn't see a thing.

I knew that bottle. There was still a little left in the bottom, not much to toss back. It was Wucheng, it burned all the way down. Don't know how long she must have carried it; holding it close to her breast really warmed it up.

I smiled. I said, Erhei, it's a good day—there's wine.

Erhei, tell me, who am I afraid of? What am I afraid of? If you're afraid of something in life, you still have to go on living; if you're afraid of nothing, you still have to go on living. Fear or no fear, there's only this one life. All you have to do is want to go on living and regardless of how much suffering and how much hardship, even if you're a horse or ox, it's still a blessing. If you don't want to go on living, you could be the emperor and eat skillet cakes and fragrant oil every day, wear an emperor's robe, ride in a sedan chair, and it would all be torture.

Isn't that so, Erhei?

Erhei buried his head in the manger and chewed, ignoring me. He was so warm, even on such a cold night, he was so warm. It really was Wucheng, it burned all the way down, burned till your head spun. It was so dark; you couldn't move it or disperse it.

Who am I afraid of? I'm not afraid at all. Isn't that so, Erhei? They say your soul remains after you die. Is that the case, Erhei? Yes or no? Tell me, Erhei.

You . . . you . . . you're so warm.

18

It was so dark you couldn't see a thing. I heard her footsteps, so I stopped her. I said, Stop, I have something to say to you.

She stopped suddenly beside me and said, You scared the hell out of me.

I raised my head and said, I have something to say to you.

She said, What's going on with you guys tonight? If you're not laying me, you're chasing me. What's with you?

I said, I have something to say to you. I want to ask you if you have agreed to anything with Commune Head Liu?

It was so dark you couldn't see a thing. But I could sense her smile—her white teeth flashed. She said, If I agree to anything or not, what does it have to do with you? That's my business. Her white teeth flashing, she was like a living demon.

Keeping my head up, I said, I'm not trying to bother you; I'm just saying that that fucker is bad. I'm afraid he'll deceive you.

She actually laughed and said, How pathetic! Not one of you can speak the truth, but you want to tell me how bad someone else is. Are you afraid that all of you runts together can't take him on? Are you afraid I'll leave with him and there's nothing you can do about it? Huh?

It was like being hit in the face with a stone. It was so dark it was like talking to a black wall. My neck hurt; I lowered my head and said, There's no need to be so nasty, okay? We're afraid you'll leave, we're afraid you'll leave, that's why we've taken care of you; we can't be grateful enough for you. Tell me, have we treated you badly in all these years at Stunted Flats?

It was so dark it was like talking to a black wall. The black wall wasn't saying anything now, nor was it smiling, nor was it throwing stones. I felt like I'd been standing in this blackness for ages. *Fuck it all to hell.*

I said, Say something! Have we mistreated you?

She didn't speak or smile. She left me on the black ground and walked away. I felt she was about to cry. *That woman!*

I said, I've been standing in the dark and the cold all day waiting for you to say something. Are you going to say anything?

All I heard in the dark was the sound of a door shutting. Someone's dog barked in the distance. A shooting star fell across the sky and was immediately drowned in the darkness.

I left; I went home. *Oh, that woman!*

In days of yore was a woman named Meng Jiangnu.
Espoused she was to a man named Fan Xilang.
Their troth the two had just pledged when
Qinshihuang dispatched the man Fan to the border.
So distraught was Meng that no food or drink crossed her lips,
Fretting for fear that her man Fan was lonely and sad.

There were no drums and no one to accompany with wooden clappers. It was so dark it was like singing to a black wall. Ugly Baby's grandpa sat on the stone roller and said, The coming of the Japanese was a disaster, but villagers, don't commit suicide. Oh, women. My mom said that year I was seven years old. The year I was seven, I led Lanzi and on the threshing ground saw Huatou, whose legs had been chopped off, and I saw my grandpa on the sacred old tree at the entrance to the village. In Ugly Baby's courtyard I saw the village women all naked, all standing white, the sun sizzling on the back of my head.

> On the thirteenth of the ninth month a cold frost fell.
> She set off to take clothes to her husband;
> Warm clothes on her back, she set off for the Great Wall,
> But nowhere was her man Fan to be seen.
> Everyone spoke, they all said
> The man Fan had long since passed away.
> Hearing their words, Meng Jiangnu's soul was grieved.
> She climbed the wall, weeping for her husband,
> Until the wall crumbled
> Revealing her man Fan's bones.

A whole courtyard full of naked women, standing, white . . . the sun sizzling on the back of his head. Ugly Baby's grandpa said, If you all put an end to your lives, who will bear babies for Stunted Flats? Oh, women . . . Aihaihaihai . . .
Fuck it all to hell!

19

Dad, sleep over here—she wet the *kang* again!

20

Brightly, brightly shone the sun on the paper of the window.

He put away the little red book and said, Okay, did you clearly hear the two lines I just read from the quotations of Chairman Mao? I said, Yes. Tianzhu snickered to himself. He said, Then repeat to me what Chairman Mao says. I said, There are only two lines. One line says we can in no way be negligent; the other says if we are going to sweep, we must sweep clean. Tianzhu just smiled and said, Okay, Kugen'r, ask what you want to ask. He won't remember. It's like driving a duck onto a perch—it's beyond him. You may as well ask Erhei. Again, he took out that little red book and said, Tianzhu, be more serious, is this any time to laugh? He opened the little red book and said, Okay, I'll read it to you again: Chairman Mao instructs us thusly: "Everything reactionary is the same; if you don't hit it, it won't fall. This is also like sweeping the floor; as a rule, where the broom does not reach, the dust will not vanish of itself." And, "Policy and tactics are the life of the Party; leading comrades at all levels must give them full attention and must never on any account be negligent." There is something else I have to tell you, and that is that the Party's strategy is "leniency for those who confess their crimes, and severity for those who refuse." Did you hear that, Cao Yongfu? Okay, explain your relationship with Qin Nuanyu. Tianzhu is head of the production team and I am head of the political team—the two of us are the leaders of Stunted Flats, understand? Okay, explain your relationship with Qin Nuanyu. Tianzhu was still snickering to himself.

I said, What relationship?

He said, You are a rich peasant, a class enemy. In your improper relationship with Nuanyu, you are confusing the class ranks in Stunted Flats. Explain now. Leniency for those who confess their crimes.

I said, What is improper? She lives in her cave and I live in my stable. Is that improper? Also, you've never told me about those class ranks of yours, and I've never seen them, so how can I confuse them?

He said, You had best make things clear—how many times have you slept with Nuanyu? What have you said to Nuanyu?

What are you talking about? Fortunately, Erhei can't understand you—what you're saying is disgraceful. I said, What is this all about? Who is going to confess to such a thing? Kugen'r, you are not married, and you don't know what is going on here. Who would say such a thing to anyone? Don't you have any shame? That's no better than being an animal, is it?

He said, Resistance will only make things worse.

I said, Worse or better, I won't say. Tianzhu, you're insulting people.

He said, Cao Yongfu, are you resisting? Let me tell you that this is class struggle. Chairman Mao says, "The revolution is not a dinner party, it is violent, it is the violent overthrow of one class by another." Cao Yongfu, we're not here today for a dinner party; you must in all honesty explain things! Once we have your confession, we will pursue more complicated issues.

Tianzhu winked at me.

I said, Tianzhu, Kugen'r, I don't know what you're up to, but for better or worse, I won't tell you anything. I'm not going to join you and insult Nuanyu. What kind of person insults a woman? Besides, Nuanyu has suffered enough in her life, so I won't join you in insulting her.

He said, Nuanyu is a contradiction among the people; you are a contradiction between ourselves and our enemies. Why do you insist upon confusing class ranks? I'm telling you, stubborn resistance will come to no good end!

Tianzhu said, Why are you being so foolish, Uncle Gimpy? Someone now wants to take Nuanyu from Stunted Flats. Kugen'r says this is a departure from the correct revolutionary stand, complicated class struggle. If you confess, Nuanyu is still Nuanyu and will stay here in Stunted Flats. Whoever has departed from the correct stand is the one who has made a mistake. Do you understand? Listen to Kugen'r and talk.

I said, I don't care who has departed and who hasn't. My stand, for better or for worse, is that I won't say anything.

Tianzhu said, You really are even worse than Erhei. Why are you so pig-headed about something so insignificant? It seems to me that you're just asking for trouble.

I said, Kugen'r, Tianzhu, if you've come here today about this, then I suggest you leave now. I have nothing to say. I still have to feed them; after eating, they still have to pull the stone roller and the millstone.

He said, Cao Yongfu, on account of this stubborn resistance of yours, we'll have to mobilize the dictatorship of the proletariat against you and convene a mass struggle meeting to struggle against you!

Tianzhu said, Good Uncle Gimpy, hurry up and speak and let me help you, okay?

He said, Tianzhu, take a firmer class stand. What are you doing? You can't talk to a rich peasant in such a way.

I said, You guys had better leave. For better or for worse, I won't say anything. I still have to feed them. After eating, they still have to pull the stone roller and the millstone.

Tianzhu said, Uncle Gimpy, you're trying to pose as a good guy, a hero, today. And you think you can still avoid trouble for yourself?

I said, What kind of a hero does a deformed guy like me make? I'm less than a coward; I'm just a cripple from Stunted Flats. You guys can leave. They haven't eaten yet this morning. Can't you hear them champing at the manger?

He said, Cao Yongfu, think about it, we'll give you one more chance. You mustn't think that without your confession we don't have our means. Even without your confession, we can continue to pursue this matter to the end. Chairman Mao says, "The golden monkey fights with a staff weighing a thousand *jun*; the universe is purified for ten thousand miles." Regardless of how complicated class struggle is, we will expose class enemies, concealed or not, and in obedience to the directives of our great leader Chairman Mao, we will purify the class ranks in Stunted Flats!

I said, You guys better leave, I have to feed them.

Brightly, brightly shone the sun on the paper of the window.

Resisting or not, the sun still shines; lenient or not, when the time comes, the sky still grows dark. Isn't that so, Erhei? I would never admit of such a thing to them. If I did, then Commune Head Liu would come after me, right? Isn't that so, Erhei? *Damn, I wish I could grow another pair of legs and join you to eat and drink, and have someone to love you without anything to worry about. That would be good.*

That's the sun shining so brightly on the paper of the window.

When the sun sets, the sky grows dark. Actually, if you close your eyes, everything grows dark. When you close your eyes, even the sun is dark. Isn't that so, Erhei? They say your soul remains after you die. Is that the case, Erhei? Yes or no? Tell me.

21

I was standing behind him; the sun was shining ahead, the blinding sun shone around his black silhouette. You could smell the overpowering horsey odor on the other side of the door curtain. He shook his head and sighed. I said, What's the matter? Are you disappointed, Kugen'r?

He shook his head and said, Tianzhu, you don't understand me. All I want to do is take care of everything according to the directives of Chairman Mao. But I never expected that the level of our class enemies here would be so low. Tell me, what can be accomplished here? I really feel as if I have let down Chairman Mao and the Party. In what way am I the son of a martyr or the successor of the revolution? He wiped his face as he spoke.

I was standing behind him; the sun was shining ahead, the blinding sun shone around his black silhouette. I stood in his shadow, looking up at him as he wiped his face. I said, Look at you, you're crying, aren't you?

He said, I really feel I've let down Chairman Mao and the Party. I'm not the son of a martyr.

I said, Kugen'r, I think you've worked hard enough; who else could do what you have done the way you've done it? Insisting on forsaking the city and coming to this old mountain valley to suffer is already an accomplishment!

He said, Tianzhu, you don't understand why I am doing this.

I said, No, I don't. You're not married, either; you have no life; who knows what you want to do? Let's go to my place and eat. You don't have to go home alone again and start a fire. You see what living alone all these years can do to a person. You can't continue the revolution without eating, can you? Let's go back to my place.

He shook his head and said, Tianzhu, you don't understand me. You wouldn't understand Zhao Yingjie, either. He walked away. The sun suddenly struck me, making my eyes smart. Understanding or not at every turn, what difference does it make? And who the hell is Zhao Yingjie? The youngster really is odd and terribly stubborn. It makes you feel sorry for him.

I turned and faced the door curtain and said, See, Uncle Gimpy, you made Kugen'r cry. You think about it. Keeping Nuanyu here in Stunted Flats is the most important thing for us. You'll be making a contribution to Stunted Flats, okay? You'll just be inconvenienced for a while, okay? I'm begging you. Later, the team will find a way to compensate you; the team will give you whatever you want, okay?

He ignored me.

The sun shone on the door curtain, shone on the wall, shone warmly on my back. The courtyard was completely silent. I looked back and saw that Kugen'r had already walked to the highest point in the village—the yellow earth bank, cleaved out of the wall of which was his cave. From a distance it looked like a single eye open in the middle of the wall of yellow earth, sizing up the distance all alone. The yellow earth overflowed with the golden light of the sun, shrouding Kugen'r in a golden halo. Above the golden land was a tile-blue sky, so blue it was dizzying.

The sun shone warmly on my back. Facing the door curtain, I said, Uncle Gimpy, I'm the team head, I handle things with the whole village in mind. This is not simply a matter between the two of us—are you really willing to let Commune Head Liu take Nuanyu away from us? Can we control Commune Head Liu without Kugen'r? Think about it, okay? Uncle Gimpy, I have to take the oxen out to graze, so I can't stay here talking with you. Don't fret, just think about it.

Still he ignored me.

Kugen'r said that I don't understand him. Understand him? No mother or father, no wife, no life, he just spends all day worrying about accomplishing something. Even with accomplishments, you still have to marry and live, right? If no one in China got married or lived, there'd be no people, and then any accomplishment, no matter how big, would mean nothing. Who would the accomplishment be for? You can't give it to the Japanese. *Fuck it all to hell.*

Kugen'r stood on the highest point of yellow earth, in which there is a single dark eye, above which was the tile-blue sky, so blue it was dizzying.

That youngster!

22

I didn't hear her call and didn't know where she went.

I said, Let's go.

He said, Is that okay? What if Uncle Gimpy sees us?

I said, Every day at this time, Uncle Gimpy is at the threshing ground carrying straw. I guarantee he won't see us. Let's go!

He said, Is that okay? If Uncle Gimpy sees me and tells Dad, he'll beat the hell out of me.

I said, Then you can just die of fear, you bastard! I'm going even if you don't. When I bring back boiled beans and soy cakes, I'll be damned if I give you a bite to eat, you bastard!

He wiped the snot from his nose on his sleeve and said, If you don't give me anything to eat, I'll tell Dad.

I said, You wouldn't dare. Are you looking for a beating?

I paid no attention to him, turned, and ran off. Behind me he shouted, Brother, Brother, wait for me, wait for me.

I ignored him and kept on running. I knew very well he had to go with me. I didn't turn around to look but just said Hurry up!

We were there in a flash. There was no one at the stable, not a sound, just a bunch of house sparrows pecking around in the manure. I picked up a dirt clod and threw it at the window; the house sparrows took flight and landed on the roof, to see if things were all clear before returning to the manure.

I said, See, Second Dog, there's no one here. The donkeys have all been taken off to work. Let's go, the beans are in the pot.

I lifted the door curtain and once in the room, ran directly to the stove. I reached out and grabbed, but the beans were so hot they burned my hand, making me tremble.

Behind me, Second Dog began crying. Uncle Gimpy, Uncle Gimpy, I wouldn't do it, it was all my elder brother's doing, he told me to come. I wouldn't do it, Uncle Gimpy. Don't tell my dad. . . .

I looked up and saw Uncle Gimpy standing on the *kang*, his small stool knocked over at his feet.

I said, Uncle Gimpy . . .

Uncle Gimpy didn't say anything, nor did he turn.

I said, Uncle Gimpy . . .

Still Uncle Gimpy said nothing.

I took to my heels and ran. Second Dog was behind me shouting, Elder Brother, Elder Brother, wait for me.

I don't know how far I ran before I stopped. Behind me, Second Dog was crying. Why didn't you wait for me, why didn't you wait for me?

I pulled Second Dog toward me and said, Second Dog, did you get a good look? Was it Uncle Gimpy?

Second Dog said, Of course it was. Uncle Gimpy was standing on the *kang*. He saw us.

I took all the black beans out of my pocket and handed them to him. I said, Okay, Second Dog, don't cry. You can have the beans, eat up.

Second Dog took the beans and wiped his nose. Second Dog said, Elder Brother, there was a rope above Uncle Gimpy's head.

I said, Hurry and eat, Second Dog. Remember, we can't tell a soul.

Putting the beans in his mouth, Second Dog said, What would happen if we told?

I said, If we tell anyone, Dad will beat the hell out of us. Do you want a beating? Just remember, okay?

Second Dog said, I'll remember. Second Dog said, I finished the beans, do you have any more?

I said, No.

Second Dog said, They were really good. Brother, how come there was a rope above Uncle Gimpy's head? Why didn't he say anything? He ignored us. He didn't turn around and there was a rope above his head.

I said, Second Dog, we didn't see anything!

Second Dog said, I saw it, I saw a rope above his head. If we knew he wasn't going to chase us, we could have taken a couple more handfuls of beans. I saw a rope above his head.

I said, You're talking about it again. If you say any more, I'll beat the fucking daylights out of you. Why can't you remember that?

Second Dog looked at me without saying a thing.

Another flock of sparrows alighted beside us and hopped around. Didn't know if it was the same flock as the one by the stable. The whole village was silent; columns of smoke rose from the cave chimneys and floated away. Didn't know whose rooster was crowing far away, so muffled, on the other side of the courtyard wall, like deep underground, with someone's hands around its neck. Dad shouted, taking the oxen out on the slopes. The cowbells were heard ringing slowly, far away; the yellow backs of the oxen shone under the sun. It was like a dream.

Second Dog said that there was a rope above Uncle Gimpy's head. Why did he tie a rope around his head?

Columns of smoke floated upward and away. The house sparrows flew by and flew away. The village was quiet. For some reason, she was crying far away, Wa-wa-wa. It was like in a dream.

Second Dog wiped his nose on his sleeve again and said, Brother, we didn't see anything. Where are we going now?

I said, Home.

23

Oh, did I scare those two kids? I was trying so hard not to scare anyone, and then I went and frightened those two kids. Look at them run—they look like a couple of rabbits. Second Dog was crying—what were you crying about? Did you think Uncle Gimpy was going to beat you over a few beans? Scold you? Big Dog is cleverer, but he thinks I don't know that he always comes here to eat beans. How could I not know? Uncle Gimpy has known since the very first time you came. Nobody can fool me about coming here—I can smell who's been here. That's the only amusing thing about this poor place. Why should Uncle Gimpy care about a couple handfuls of beans? Tell me, why would he begrudge you? He fed the animals, why not you? I was trying so hard not to scare anyone and then I frightened those two kids. Dang. I can't open my mouth and say anything. You wouldn't hear . . . anyway.

After eating breakfast, they came to take them away. I said good-bye to Heini, then Laoni, then Dahei, and finally to Erhei. I rubbed his head and said, Erhei, we'll meet in the netherworld. After I'm gone, you have to do as you're told, you have to do whatever the person who comes to feed you tells you. No one will love you as much as I do. If you don't do as you're told, they'll beat you. That would make me sad, wouldn't it? Tell me, have I ever raised a hand against you? Would I do that? Listen to me, in the future work is work, just the same as when I was here. Be good, no tricks; you have to behave whether or not anyone is watching. In the future, don't always be provoking Dahei—later, who's going be around to protect you when I'm not here? Erhei blinked his eyes but said nothing. He had no idea where I was going. I untied the rope from around Erhei's neck and said, Erhei, I've loved you, and now that I'm going, I'd like to use your rope, is that okay? Erhei blinked his eyes but said nothing. I untied and removed his old rope and replaced it with a new one, along with new blinders. I said, Erhei, before I leave, I'm giving you a new set of blinders; this'll be the last time. In a while, when you return, I won't be here. You won't see me; I won't be here, that's it. Don't cry for me and don't think about me. Everyone under Heaven must die. You must die. I must die. When the living reach the end of the line, they up and die. I just hope that in the next life, I can grow two more legs and stand with you, eat and drink with you, be loved by someone. That would be great, wouldn't it? When that day comes, I'll be able to spend every day chatting with you. We can work together, eat together, and sleep together. How wonderful. Erhei flicked his ears; he understood. I laughed; after all, he's my Erhei. He knows whatever I'm thinking. *Hey, hey, he's my Erhei. My love for you has not been in vain.*

Okay, Dahei left, Heini left, Laoni left, and Erhei left. They all left, gone. I was the only one left here, left here with the rope from Erhei. I took the old one because it was soft and pliant. I didn't want to scare them. I was leaving, going away on my own.

I didn't want to frighten anyone. *Erhei still hasn't told me, is a soul left after we die? Yes or no? Erhei hasn't told me. Maybe he was guessing; maybe he didn't want me to go. Erhei, Erhei, you have no idea that when a person doesn't want to go on living, even spending every day as the emperor, riding in a sedan chair, wearing an emperor's robes, and eating skillet cakes and oil, all become torture. It's pointless. But if a person wants to go on living, regardless of how much suffering and hardship, then, even if he's a horse or an ox, it's still a blessing, and he'll be willing.* But I didn't really want to go on living; even if you made me emperor, I wouldn't be willing. *I want to see how they'll purify class ranks without me, how they'll rectify things. I want to see what'll happen to that team and classes. Where'll they be? Anything left to feed the dogs? Or will they put it in a jar and pickle it? I've lived a long time and I've seen teams, and they were the people who carried guns and killed others. What is this class thing? Is it round or square? I'm sure Erhei has no idea either. Chairman Mao is, after all, Chairman Mao, that's why he can think up things like class, but we the people can't; otherwise he wouldn't be in charge of the world. Forget it. Who cares any longer? This rope is soft and pliant and it still has Erhei's smell.* Soft and pliant, it would do. *It still has Erhei's smell. When I get there and see the king of the underworld, he'll say, Okay, you even brought the rope and all. As a favor, we'll reincarnate you as a donkey. My love has not been wasted on Erhei, even the rope is his. Soft and pliant, it'll work fine, won't it? Where could I find a better rope? Except Erhei who left it to me, who else knows me? Everything is ready. Here's my stool, all wiped off. Here's the rope, soft and pliant, and it still has Erhei's smell. Where could I find such a good rope? Oh, I am going, going. The fodder is already mixed for them, the beans are cooked, and the cistern is full of water. Everything is ready for them when they get back from work. Okay, nothing else to worry about, I am going, going. It's a pity I can't drink the wine Nuanyu gives me and see my Erhei anymore. Okay, nothing else to worry about. I am going, going. Get up on the* kang, the stool is in place, the rope hung. *This is the best place.* I spent days lying on the *kang* thinking about it and decided this was the best place. *The height is just right and no one can see it. I'm going, going. Facing inward, back to the door, I really don't want them to see my face, I don't want to scare them, I don't want to scare anyone. I'm leaving, going my own way. What's the point of scaring other people? The rope is hung, tied with a slipknot. How many years have I been leading them around on the end of a rope; today I'm at the end of the rope. I'll handle it smoothly and well. I've lived a long time and it'll be over soon. Here, put the rope over my head, get up on the stool . . . clunk . . . can't move . . . can't get loose . . . oh, it's so dark . . . I really scared those two kids. Dang. Why are you running away? I can't open my mouth. I can't say anything. That means you wouldn't hear it.*

24

When I arrived, the courtyard was already full of people. Everyone in the village was there, except for the men who'd gone out into the valley to repair the embankment. Young and old, male and female, they were all crowded outside the stable window. No meeting in the village was ever so crowded. Don't know who opened the window, but through it you could see his profile, a hemp rope up behind his ear, hanging from a beam, like some dirty clothes hanging there. The kids were all staring wide-eyed; the eyes of the women were all red; Nuanyu was leaning against the windowsill, shouting, Uncle Gimpy, Uncle Gimpy, what have you done? *That woman! She doesn't have the least bit of damned class consciousness! Who was he? What time is this? You're a poor peasant. What are you crying for?*

I pushed my way through the crowd and said, What are you all looking at? Why don't you hurry up and take him down? Hurry up!

No one dared move.

I grabbed the axe from the woodpile and said, Move aside. Who's afraid of a dead man? I've seen plenty of dead people!

I carried the axe inside and stood on the *kang*, face to face with him. I never looked so close at him before; in the past I always had to look down on him. Now he was hanging from a beam, a head taller than before. People say that the tongue of a person who hangs himself will stick out. Not his. There was no life left in his face, whiter than in the past. I said, Cao Yongfu, I only transmitted the central documents yesterday, and today you hang yourself! What the hell were you afraid of? Does anyone still think that class struggle in Stunted Flats is not complicated? I swung the axe at the beam. The accumulated dust fell from the beam, getting in my eyes. Although my eyes were filled with dust, I saw him drop stiffly to the *kang*, standing right in front of me without moving. I quickly rubbed my eyes and said, Cao Yongfu . . . but without making a sound, he fell against my chest. Everyone in the courtyard cried out in a single voice. By the time I could see, he had slipped down to my belly. I said, Gimpy Five, what the fuck were you thinking? When Political Commissar Wang fell against me, his chest was covered with blood. He opened his eyes and smiled and said, Little devil . . . Gimpy Five, what the hell were you thinking? . . . Little devil . . . I tell you, Gimpy Five, I'm a Communist and don't believe in this nonsense of yours.

I put him down on the *kang* and returned to the courtyard. I said, The situation demands an investigation. I said, Who was the first to find him? Ugly Baby's wife said she was the first to see him when she brought the donkey back from turning the millstone. Ugly Baby's wife said, I shouted but no one responded. I lifted the door curtain and came in, and my soul nearly jumped out of me. I said, Okay, just tell me the facts, and none of that superstitious talk about souls. That's feudal superstition. Ugly Baby's wife said, Anyway, I nearly gave up my soul; it nearly scared me to death. Looking at the others, I said, Anything else? No? Then he committed suicide, he alienated himself from the people. Two dirty kids squeezed up front, faces upraised. The little one said, We didn't see anything; we just came to eat a handful of cooked beans. . . . The bigger one shoved him and said, You're itching for a damned beating! I said, Go away, kids should only be seen and not heard when adults are talking. Who'll go to the valley and tell the people working there to come back? Who'll go get Tianzhu, who's out grazing the oxen? The bigger kid said, I'll go get my dad. I said, Oh, you're Big Dog. The little one said, I'll go with my elder brother. I said, Oh, you're Second Dog. Okay, go, and make it fast! Tell them that I said Gimpy Five killed himself and that everyone must return and no one needs to work. This issue must be dealt with. The bigger kid opened his eyes wide and said, You fool, I'm not going to fucking take you! The little one rubbed his face and cried, If you don't take me, I'll tell Dad. . . . I said, Okay, okay, take him for the sake of unity. I waved my hand at the people in the courtyard and said, Okay, everyone leave, don't hang around here. There's nothing to see when a rich peasant kills himself. Get going.

Nuanyu said, Uncle Gimpy has to be dressed in a new set of clothes. As she spoke, the tears ran down her face.

That woman! She has no sense of class stand at all!

I said, Don't talk so much. This is a political issue, what's a woman doing getting foolishly mixed up in it?

Nuanyu paid no attention to me and said, Whatever, but he still needs to be dressed in a new set of clothes. If you're not going to do it, I will!

That woman! She's like an animal, wooden headed; there's no point in thinking you can reason with her.

I waved my hand and said, Okay, get the hell out of here, you fucking cunts! You're not a bunch of sheep that have to have someone come and shoo you away, are you? There's nothing to see when a rich peasant kills himself. Get going.

The crowd dispersed, trickling away like a flock of sheep. Soon, all that was left in the courtyard were the four donkeys, tethered to the hitching post. Uncle Gimpy was laid out on the *kang*. You could see his face through the window, a white face on an old, dirty quilt, a white face with no life left in it.

One of the donkeys dug at the ground with its front hoof, *dig, thud, dig, thud, dig, thud, dig, thud*, it was enough to drive a person mad! I scolded it, What are you digging for? Do you fucking want to hang yourself too? That black donkey kept at it, *dig, thud, dig, thud, dig, thud*; suddenly it lifted its head and brayed deafeningly!

What the hell are you braying about? What an animal!

25

My ancestors! My hands were trembling so much I couldn't light the lamp.

I placed the lamp made of half a hollowed-out potato on the stove, poured some oil in, and, as Uncle San told me, put in twenty-nine wicks, cut a person out of paper and placed it in the bottom of the cistern, placed a *sheng* of rice before the lamp, and then cut some paper banners to stick in the grain. As I cut the paper, I cut my finger with the scissors; the blood ran and ran, but I couldn't look after it. I found three sticks of incense and stuck them in the rice as well. With a burning hemp stalk, I tried to light the lamp. My ancestors, I was trembling so much I couldn't light it.

My ancestors! Even now my two legs are still weak. My ancestors, it scared me. How many times? He never caught me before, just this time he caught me for sure! I called the ghost. Why on earth did I have to do it today? If I'd known he was hanging there, you could have beaten me and I wouldn't have gone there. Every day he went to the threshing ground at this time to collect the dry straw. I knew he wasn't there. I tethered Laoni to the hitching post and listened, but didn't hear a thing. I said, Uncle Gimpy, I brought the donkey back. I didn't hear a sound, and I know that every day at this time he is gone. I went in—how many times had I taken some? The pot for the corn was there in the corner. I pulled off the slab and loaded up my pockets, then replaced the slab, about to leave. I turned, and that's when I saw him. I fell to my knees before him. I started to cry and said, Uncle Gimpy, Uncle Gimpy, Uncle Gimpy, I was wrong, I shouldn't steal the team's corn; this is the only time I ever stole any, you caught me red-handed. But you can't say anything—if you do, how could I ever face the villagers? Uncle Gimpy, I said, I'll do anything you say, but just don't tell anyone. I'll kowtow to you, Uncle Gimpy, I'll kowtow to you. I bowed, and when I lifted my head I saw as clear as day that he was hanging from a beam. I was so scared that I fell back on the ground. My legs were weak and my pants were wet. . . . I said, Uncle Gimpy, Uncle Gimpy, what have you done? My legs were so weak I couldn't stand up. My pants were all wet. I got up off the ground.

My ancestors, just this one time I had to let him catch me. So many times and I never had a problem; just that one time I had to let him catch me. Even now my two legs are still weak. Big Commune Head, what do you need a soul for? You have one, don't you? Every day you make public money, you eat and drink well. What do you need a soul for? But I can't lose my soul—who'll cook for my big family? Who'll wait on Ugly Baby, who'll feed the chickens, who'll feed the pigs? Who'll collect the eggs the chickens lay? Who'll wash the clothes when they get dirty? Who'll patch the clothes when they tear? I can't lose my soul—I still want to hold my grandchildren.

I barred the door and while no one was around, I hurried and did it so that I could quickly see off Uncle Gimpy. I should have asked Uncle San over to do this, but I didn't have a chance to talk with him today. How would I put it? I'd say, Uncle San, today I went over to the stable to steal some corn and ran into Uncle Gimpy. I'm afraid Uncle Gimpy will come for my soul; could you see him off for me?

Goodness, my hands were trembling so much I couldn't light the lamp.

Okay, it was done. I knelt for Uncle Gimpy. Of all the verses Uncle San intoned for the dead, I couldn't remember even one. *I remember "One thousand rising spirits; ten thousand rising spirits," but I can't remember what comes after. Uncle Gimpy, you'll have to make do; I'll kowtow to you, Uncle Gimpy. "One thousand rising spirits; ten thousand rising spirits." Good people won't remember the faults of their inferiors; Uncle Gimpy, you'll just have to spare me this time. "One thousand rising spirits; ten thousand rising spirits." Uncle Gimpy, tomorrow I'll go and cry for you, tomorrow I'll go and make offerings to you, but whatever you do, don't come for my soul. "One thousand rising spirits; ten thousand rising spirits." Uncle Gimpy, if you can't have pity on me, you must have pity on my kids and Ugly Baby. "One thousand rising spirits; ten thousand rising spirits." Uncle Gimpy, in the future I'll visit your grave on Tomb-Sweeping Festival, I'll burn spirit money for you; when it's cold I'll take you warm clothes; when it's warm, I'll take you cool clothes. "One thousand rising spirits; ten thousand rising spirits." Uncle Gimpy, I'll never steal again, I wouldn't dare; if I do, may my hands rot and may I go blind. "One thousand rising spirits; ten thousand rising spirits." Uncle Gimpy, Uncle Gimpy, I don't believe in any god, but I believe in you; I beg you, Uncle Gimpy, I'm kowtowing, I'll cry until I go blind, please take pity on my kids and Ugly Baby. "One thousand rising spirits; ten thousand rising spirits." Uncle Gimpy, I know that's the food for Erhei and the others; I know you love them more than yourself and I know you treat them better than you'd treat your own kids. I oppress animals that can't talk—I'm worse than an animal. Uncle Gimpy, please spare me, aiya, aiya, aiya. . . . "One thousand rising spirits; ten thousand rising spirits."*

So many yellow ones so many yellow ones so many yellow ones so many yellow ones milling around

So many yellow ones, scattering

This black one this black one this black one this black one stays and howls like a wolf

The green one is inside the green one is inside the green one is inside the green one is silent want to see the green one *thud* want to go in want to see the green one *thud* want to go in *thud* want to go in *thud thud thud thud* the green one is mine the green one is mine *thud* the green one is mine *thud* the green one is inside the green one is inside *thud thud thud thud*

Ee-aw, ee-aw, ee . . . aw

So many yellow ones scattering the black one stays the green one is inside

Ee-aw, ee-aw, ee . . . aw

The green one is inside

The green one is silent the green one is inside

The green one is mine ee-aw, ee-aw, ee . . . aw *thud, thud, thud, thud, thud*

I removed the black cloth and the cotton from the cabinet and spread the cloth on the *kang*. When I'd finished cutting out the shirt and pants, she came in holding a bundle wrapped in cloth.

She'd been crying and her eyes were red. She said, Nuanyu, use my cloth to make clothes for Uncle Gimpy.

I said, Look, I've already cut them out. Shell, lining, and cotton.

She said, Nuanyu, better use mine.

I said, Look, I've already cut them out. Besides, you have a big family and you haven't made any winter clothes yet. Using this cloth, what'll you do for the kids' clothes? From the looks of it, Ugly Baby's wearing a shabby quilted jacket.

She said, Your clothes are old too.

I said, But I don't have a family, so that's easy to take care of.

She said, Why do you think Uncle Gimpy did it? Huh? Huh?

She cried. When she cried, I started.

I said, We shouldn't cry. Better be quick about this—Uncle Gimpy is still waiting for his clothes.

She said, Okay, no tears. Uncle Gimpy was so sad all his life; he had nothing but those donkeys . . .

She started in again, so I began to cry too.

I said, Really, no more tears; any more and we'll upset Uncle Gimpy.

She climbed up on the *kang*, picked up needle and thread, and started plying it with her fingers. She wiped away her tears and said, You have no idea—when I saw him I was scared out of my wits, so scared I wet my pants. Why do you think Uncle Gimpy did it?

I said, There was no reason. When someone's life is no better than that of a donkey, why the hell go on living? One day I'll do the same as him and hang myself. It's better to die than live a life with no meaning.

She sucked in the cold air and opened her eyes wide. She said, Nuanyu, you scare me. Look, I've pricked myself with the needle! What are you saying? You're young and not deformed like us. What are you saying? What's wrong with me today? I keep running into such scary things.

She cried; I cried. Finally, I said, Don't cry, don't cry; if we keep crying, we'll never finish Uncle Gimpy's clothes.

After working a bit, I couldn't help myself; I said, Last night, after the meeting, I saw him at the stable.

Her eyes widened. Last night?

I knew what she was thinking. I said, Yes, last night.

She said, What did you do, going there in the middle of the night, a woman all alone?

I knew what she was thinking. I said, I went there at midnight to take him some liquor.

She said, You took him liquor, all alone in the middle of the night?

I knew what she was thinking. I said, After the meeting last night, Uncle Gimpy didn't say anything, not one word; even when I poured water for him, he didn't dare drink it. I was afraid something was wrong, so I followed him. First he stood by the wall of the Earth God's temple for a while and waited until everyone else had left before going back to the stable. I thought something would happen to him, so I followed him. I followed him to the stable, where I gave him the liquor.

She said, What did he say to you?

I knew what she was thinking. I said, Uncle Gimpy, you don't have to be afraid of anything, but he didn't say anything except insist that I should hurry home, hurry home. If I'd known he was thinking of hanging himself, I wouldn't have listened to him and I wouldn't have left.

She said, A woman all by yourself, certainly you couldn't have stayed at his place all night. You'd have had to go and get someone.

I put down my sewing and said, Ugly Baby's woman, I know what you're thinking. I also know what you want to say. You're thinking that it's not right for a woman, a widow, to be alone with a poor unmarried man; you're saying that there's no reason for a man and the woman to spend the night together except for doing that, right? Let me tell you that I'm not afraid of what you say about me. If I were afraid, I wouldn't be alive today! If I were afraid, I would have hanged myself long ago. I would have long since rotted in the ground. I really regret not spending last night at Uncle Gimpy's; I really regret not having slept with Uncle Gimpy last night. If I had slept there, how could he have hanged himself? It's so pitiful, pitiful in the extreme when a person doesn't want to live, when they reach the point where they want to die. What can you give him for that life of his? What can you give him? Even if you gave him a mountain of gold and silver, it wouldn't be enough; it'd be useless! I really regret not spending last night at Uncle Gimpy's. If

I'd slept there, he might still be alive. I'm not afraid. I've been at Stunted Flats for so many years, who doesn't know what I am here? What am I afraid of? Hell, I'm the same as Uncle Gimpy now—I'm not even afraid to die! The only person in Stunted Flats who really cared for me was Uncle Gimpy, no one else. I don't want him to be dead; I want to sleep with him. Say something. If you want to say something, go ahead. Hurry up and say what's on your mind.

She stopped sewing and said, Nuanyu, look at you, what are your crying about? What did I say about you? I didn't say anything, did I? Doesn't everyone know you saved our men here at Stunted Flats? The men here do not have good consciences, but does that mean the women here are the same? I tell you, I want to be a man in my next life and want all these men to come back as women. Then I'll humiliate them, walk all over them the way you would a pig or a dog, I'll humiliate them to death! I want to live a long time and live two hundred damn years, so that every one of them will be afraid of me!

We cried together and talked. Then we said, Don't cry, let's not say any more, Uncle Gimpy is still waiting on his clothes. As we were crying and talking, he pushed open the door and came in. Staring straight at me, he said, So that's the way it was, damn you! I knew there was something between you and Uncle Gimpy. A woman like you has no class stand at all!

I said, I'm glad you know. I was afraid you didn't know.

He slapped his thigh and said, Nuanyu, Nuanyu, what can I say about you?

She got off the *kang*. She looked at me, then at him, and said, If you have something to say to each other, I'll leave.

I knew what she was thinking. I said, Don't go, Ugly Baby's woman, we haven't talked yet. Let's get back to work—Uncle Gimpy's waiting for his clothes. I said, You can leave, we don't need a man standing around getting in the way while we women work. Go on, get out of here.

28

Brother! Brother! Brother, it's a whirlwind, a whirlwind! He shouted from behind, Brother, a whirlwind's coming!

The road, tramped white, curved over the plateau, twisting like a white snake up out of the valley. The whirlwind twisted like a writhing black snake above the road, heading directly toward us along that white belt.

He shouted from behind, Brother, Uncle Gimpy said that whirlwinds are walking ghosts. Brother, I'm scared!

Looking at the whirlwind as it twisted toward us, I said, Don't be afraid, Second Dog, let me carry you.

It twisted toward us. My brother held me. The blowing dirt got in my eyes.

Uncle Gimpy said, Big Dog, Second Dog.

He just shouted, Brother, Uncle Gimpy is speaking! Uncle Gimpy is calling us!

I said, Uncle Gimpy, Uncle Gimpy, we hear you.

Uncle Gimpy said, Big Dog, Second Dog, you are good kids. Children, remember what I tell you.

I said, Uncle Gimpy, if you have something to say, just say it.

Uncle Gimpy said, Big Dog, Second Dog, tell your dad to bury Uncle Gimpy at Fifteen Mu. Got it?

I said, Got it, Uncle Gimpy. Bury Uncle Gimpy at Fifteen Mu.

The whirlwind released us and twisted away.

Second Dog let go of me and shot off like a streak of lightning, screaming, Uncle Gimpy, Uncle Gimpy, Uncle Gimpy, we didn't see a thing, all we did was eat a handful of cooked beans! If we'd known you wouldn't come after us, my brother would have taken a couple more handfuls!

I scolded him, You fool, get back here right now. Do you want to lose your fucking soul?

Pouting, he came back muttering, I heard Uncle Gimpy talk; I just wanted to see him. Isn't he at the stable? How could he come with us?

I scolded him, You're a motherfucking fool. You don't know anything. Uncle Gimpy is dead, he's become a ghost. If you chase after a ghost, it'll catch you up and carry off your soul. Then you won't even fucking be able to go home. Then where would I go to find you? You're so damned dumb, you little bastard! Saying anything to you is a waste of breath, you don't understand anything at all! Hurry up and come along with me.

Pouting, he followed behind me. The road twisted like a snake up out of the valley. I looked back and saw that Uncle Gimpy was gone, nowhere in sight, having left behind a few dry yellow leaves on the road.

I said, Second Dog, don't be angry, hurry up and come along with me. Do you remember what Uncle Gimpy just said?

Second Dog said, Yes, I remember. Uncle Gimpy said to tell Dad that he should bury him at Fifteen Mu. Brother, why do you think Uncle Gimpy wants to be buried there?

I said, Second Dog, don't talk about it; let's go. I don't know why either.

Dry yellow leaves littered the ground. There wasn't a breath of wind, there wasn't a patch of cloud, there wasn't a sound or shadow. Where did Uncle Gimpy come from? Was he really dead or not?

I said, Let's go, Second Dog.

Second Dog nodded and said, Let's go.

I said, Second Dog, are you afraid?

Second Dog said, No. I just want to see Uncle Gimpy. Second Dog said, Brother, are you afraid?

I said, No.

Second Dog said, Brother, Uncle Gimpy is dead but he can still talk. If we died tomorrow and became whirlwinds and could go wherever we want and talk in the wind too, would the villagers be afraid?

I said, Second Dog, don't talk such foolishness. If you do, Uncle Gimpy might come back.

Second Dog turned to look back and said, He's not there, where is he?

The dry yellow leaves littered the ground without moving. The twisting road descended from under our feet to the valley below, like a big snake lying on the ground.

Was Uncle Gimpy really dead or not?

There wasn't a breath of wind, there wasn't a patch of cloud, there wasn't a sound or shadow. Deep in the bottom of the valley, the people of Leiba looked like ants crawling around on the ground. The oxen on the north-facing slope, with yellow backs and pointed horns, seemed to emerge and disappear again above the thickets. Dad looked like an ant; he was carrying the small shovel he took when herding the oxen, following the river down into the valley. Where did Uncle Gimpy come from? Dry yellow leaves littered the ground without moving.

I said, Let's go, Second Dog.

29

I stood outside the door, so angry I could hardly breathe. *That woman! Ten thousand generations wouldn't be long enough to figure out what she is going to do!* This was the first time in my life I had ever been thrown out by a woman, the first time in my life I had ever looked so damned bad! *Get out! Leave! I'm going to the stable to see that lover of yours!*

It's still digging, dig thud dig thud dig thud dig.... *What the hell are you digging for? You beast! Tell me, Uncle Gimpy, as a cripple, how can you compare with me at all? He just lies there without moving. You can see his face through the window, a white face amid the dark shadows, so white and bloodless.* When he dropped from the beam, it was that face looking at me, as if he wanted to open his eyes once more. When Political Commissar Wang fell in my arms, his chest was covered with blood; his face was just as white and bloodless, white as a sheet of paper. Political Commissar Wang opened his eyes and looked at me. He smiled and said, Little devil. . . . *I survived a hail of bullets and walked out from a pile of corpses. Am I scared of you? Tell me, how can a cripple like you compare with me at all?* It's still digging, dig, thud, dig, thud . . . *you beast! Do you think I can't marry Nuanyu? Do you think you can stop me? Why don't you stand up, look at me, and see who I am? I am Director Liu! I am Liu Changsheng! In this place, what I say goes. Do you understand? I have spent a lifetime in the revolution and will risk it for the truth. Uncle Gimpy, you fucker, why did you contradict the truth spoken by Nuanyu? How could you be so fucking disgusting? You really are a class enemy—you ruined everything I care about. How could you be so on target?* It's still digging, dig, thud, dig, thud, dig, thud. . . . *I'm going to slaughter you, you damned beast! I noticed that there was something wrong with you last night. When I was transmitting the central documents, Nuanyu poured some water for you— the class stand of a good poor peasant totally fucking messed up by a rich peasant. If the class ranks are not purified, you will change the color of Stunted Flats. Chairman Mao is great. Without Chairman Mao's directives, how could we purify such a big problem? How would we know that class enemies, rich peasants, are so savage? Damn it, what are you digging for?* Dig, thud, dig, thud, thud, thud, thud. . . .

You don't think I'll marry Nuanyu, do you? Get real! Nuanyu is a part of my heart. Don't think you're going to dig your way out of here! Dig, thud, dig, thud, dig, thud. . . . *Don't think you're going to dig your way out of here. I'm going back to the commune tomorrow. It's nothing for me to write out a divorce certificate. I'll stand in the commune courtyard and call Secretary Sun and have him write any number of divorce certificates; I could divorce eighteen times if I wished. Rest in peace, Uncle Gimpy, and let your beast dig away. I'll show you whose wife Nuanyu will be. That's my stand, and I, Liu Changsheng, want to see who can stop me!*

30

I saw them come running from a distance. Before they got to me, they were already shouting confusedly, Dad, Dad, Dad, don't graze the oxen hurry and take them back we didn't see anything we only ate a handful of boiled beans later Uncle Gimpy died Commune Head Liu said you have to go back and take care of the matter there was a rope above Uncle Gimpy's head Commune Head Liu cut him down with an axe everyone in the village saw him he used an axe to cut down Uncle Gimpy he fell, Dad, Dad, Dad, hurry and return to the village with the oxen. . . .

I thrust the shovel into the ground and said, Quit your damned shouting and one of you tell me what's going on, one of you tell me!

The two little bastards were out of breath, so I scolded them. Now neither one of them wanted to talk. I'm telling you, talk!

Big Dog said, Dad, Uncle Gimpy is dead.

Second Dog said, Dad, there was a rope above Uncle Gimpy's head.

Big Dog said, Commune Head Liu says that Uncle Gimpy killed himself.

Second Dog said, Dad, we didn't se anything, we just ate a handful of boiled beans, there was a rope above Uncle Gimpy's head, later Commune Head Liu cut him down with an axe.

I felt dizzy, so I sat down on the rock behind me. I said, Uncle Gimpy, why did you take things to heart? It's like I killed you with my own hands, isn't it? You might want to die, but you can't die this way! What's the matter with you? Fuck it all to hell! Why couldn't you just take it?

Big Dog said, Dad, Commune Head Liu said that Uncle Gimpy killed himself. It wasn't you who killed him.

Second Dog said, Dad, we saw it, there was a rope above Uncle Gimpy's head. When there was a rope above his head, you were setting off for the slope with the oxen.

I shook my head and said, No, you don't know what I'm talking about. Kids, don't go back to the village right now—go to Nanliu Village and tell Uncle Chuandeng and Erniu to come and make a coffin for Uncle Gimpy. Tell them I said so. Money's not a problem; tell him whatever he wants, Stunted Flats will pay. Tell him the wood is ready and is all drying in the sheep pen; it's been drying for four or five years. You got that?

The two kids nodded their heads.

I said, After the coffin is finished, we'll bury Uncle Gimpy at Fifteen Mu, which he requested plenty of times.

The two kids were wide-eyed. Big Dog said, Dad, did Uncle Gimpy come looking for you too? And tell you he wanted to be buried at Fifteen Mu?

I said, What are you talking about? Were you scared out of your wits?

Second Dog said, Dad, just a while ago Uncle Gimpy told us that he wanted to be buried at Fifteen Mu. How come you know too? Did he come to you as a whirlwind too?

I waved my hand and said, Okay, you two, don't talk nonsense to me. Is this any time for that? Hurry up, hurry up. Oh yeah, Big Dog, here's two *yuan*. Go to the commissary and buy a carton of Greenleaf cigarettes for this business of Uncle Gimpy's.

Remember, one *mao* four *fen* a pack, one *yuan* four for a carton; you'll get six *mao* in change, nothing less. If you come back short, I'll give the two of you a fucking beating. Remember, come back with Uncle Chuandeng and Erniu, the sooner the better. I'll be waiting for you at the village. Hurry up and get going!

Watching them run off, I still couldn't get to my feet. *Fuck it all to hell! I've never felt so confused in all my life.* My mouth felt so dry, I could've blown smoke. There wasn't any wind. The white sun shone warmly on the water trickling in the valley bottom. Early in the morning, a thin layer of ice formed along the edges, leaving just a trickle, the winter water flowing feebly without a sound. If it weren't for the reflected sunlight, you'd never know the water was moving. The sound of cow bells, neither hurried nor slow, faded in and out of the thickets. The world was still the same world, but Uncle Gimpy was no longer in it. I glanced at the white sun; I glanced at the silent water, cool and clear. I moved from the rock and walked to the riverbank. First I grasped the shovel, then shifted it from hand to hand, slowly lowering myself to the ground; then, supporting myself with my two hands, I lowered my head, like an ox, to the water, my legs and waist unbent. Being a cripple is worse than being a cow. I thrust my head into the icy river water. Immediately an excruciating pain shot through my face, everything went black before my eyes, and it was cold inside my mouth. Uncle Gimpy was no longer in this world. Uncle Gimpy . . . it was no longer the same world. The sound of cow bells, neither hurried nor slow, faded in and out of the thickets, as if from the bottom of the river, as if from the dark reaches of the underworld. I pulled my face out of the icy water; drops of water ran steadily from my chin and cheeks. The white sun hung high above my back. The sun was still here, the oxen were still here, the water was still here, but Uncle Gimpy was not. When I was seven, the Japs came. My mom couldn't carry me, so Uncle Gimpy did. My mom was gone, so was my dad, and now so was Uncle Gimpy. The wind was still here, blowing on my face—a sudden chill on my face.

31

I counted, sixty-eight, sixty-nine, seventy, seventy-one, seventy-two . . . what was it that kept splashing on my face? I couldn't let go—I had to hold the rock drill. Eighty-three, eighty-four, eighty-five, eighty-six . . . what was it that kept splashing on my face? I saw that the hammer handle was all red. I shouted, Stop! Look at your hands!

He didn't stop. He said, Ugly Baby, don't let go, we said one hundred. Then he picked up the count, ninety-eight, ninety-nine, one-hundred!

Only when he reached one hundred did he stop swinging that eighteen-pound sledge. Sweat rained from his head, heat rose from his scalp. It was more like the hottest days of summer than the coldest days of winter.

Quick, take a look at your hands.

He opened his hands and I saw that they were covered with blood; I saw a bloody red hand. He smiled and said, It's nothing, just a little blood.

I said, You're going to kill yourself, take a break.

Still smiling, he said, My worn-out hands indicate that I'm still not sufficiently tempered. I need to strengthen myself with more striking and polishing!

I hurried over to the fire and grabbed a handful of wood ash and sprinkled it on his hands. Only when I grabbed that bloody hand of his did I realize it was trembling. I pressed his hand to my chest and said, Kugen'r, Kugen'r, what is this all about? Are you trying to kill yourself? All of us cripples together can't do all the work, how do you expect to do it alone? You're only human. Your hands are made of flesh, aren't they? What are you doing? No matter what, I can't let you continue today. You go home at once!

He was still smiling. He said, Ugly Baby, why are you crying? Is there a revolution where blood doesn't flow? If we can change the face of Stunted Flats, a little blood is nothing. I'd willingly sacrifice myself!

I pressed the ash into his hand and said, I don't like to hear that sort of talk. Sacrificing someone comes too easily. If we're talking sacrifice, let a couple more of these cripples sacrifice themselves. Life is suffering, life is a burden.

He snatched back his hand and said, I've already planned it. Our Stunted Flats has a total of twelve valleys, big and small. On average, one can be put in order every two years, and it will take twenty-four years to put them all in order. By then we'll plant grain on the good flat land in the valley and on the slopes construct fish-scale pits for holding water, and build terraces and plant fruit trees. . . .

I continued, We'll build a hydroelectric station, build a small school—you can be the teacher and the principal . . . you must've said all this eighty times. It's all a dream, right?

His eyes lit up like two lanterns in the middle of the day. He said, Ugly Baby, it's not a dream.

I said, By the time all that happens, how old will you be? Eighty? Ninety?

He said, It doesn't matter. We'll build an old-folks home and all of us old people will live there. There'll be a doctor and a nurse; there'll be nothing to worry about—there'll be someone to take care of our food and clothes.

I said, Why, of course, it'll be no different from an emperor living in a golden palace. If it's not a dream, what is it? There's only one emperor under Heaven—if everyone wants to be emperor, isn't that a dream? Besides, won't the earthworks we built the first two years be swept away as soon as the water from the mountains increases? Where are we going to find good flat land? Things only get worse when man opposes or contests with Heaven, so will there be any fruit to eat? Other than eating a few extra rations and wasting some energy, what else will we get? Tell me!

He said, We must possess the spirit of the Foolish Old Man who moved the mountains. We mustn't retreat the moment we encounter difficulty.

I said, In the end, didn't the Foolish Old Man have help from the immortals? Who do we have? Other than you, the only person of sound body, there are only cripples. Everyone is a damned cripple. If all of us cripples damn well became the Foolish Old Man, we'd all be just a bunch of crippled foolish old men and nothing would get done.

My words immediately extinguished those two lamps. He shook his head and said, None of you understands me; none of you understands what I am really doing. He turned to measure up that patch of stone at his feet. He said, Ugly Baby, Chairman Mao says, "Wherever there is struggle there is sacrifice, and death is a common occurrence." Sometimes I'd like to sacrifice myself to show all of you. If I sacrificed myself, then you would understand what I am really doing, you would know what it is I'm thinking. After six years, I realize more clearly than ever why sacrifice is happiness to some people. None of you can understand what I am saying; it'll never be clear to you. If one person dies, nothing will get done, but only at death can a person truly and finally accomplish everything he has thought about doing. None of you knows the meaning of the word "ideal"—that's my duty. Chairman Mao says, "The serious problem is the education of the peasantry." But sometimes I think the only way any of you will ever understand the word "ideal" is through the sacrifice of one person. This is my duty. I should be like all revolutionary martyrs and awaken the masses with my own blood, shake the people from their numbness. It's my duty. One day I will accomplish this; one day I will accomplish everything I want. I want to accomplish everything Zhao Yingjie is capable of.

The sun was in my eyes. I looked up, and all I could see was the back of his head as he faced that patch of stone while grasping the handle of the hammer stained with his blood. His hair looked like a mess of grass on account of his previous strenuous exertions, and now under the sun it glowed as if it had caught fire. That pile of stones seemed to have understood what he said, because the hole just opened also shone under the sun. I really felt like an ignorant beast, like a wooden post. I vaguely felt that what he said must be good educated words, but I damned well couldn't figure out what he was talking about. He stood tall and large under the sun, the messy grass on top of his head burning like flames, the patch of stone before us also glowing like fire.

I said, Kugen'r, does your hand still hurt?

He didn't look around.

I said, Kugen'r, does your hand still hurt?

Still he did not turn around. He said, Ugly Baby, go tell the others to take shelter in the cave while I plant the dynamite.

His wild hair was enflamed under the high sun. The bloody hammer handle stood upright and motionless, next to which, in the distance, I could see Tianzhu running toward us. He was shouting, Kugen'r, Kugen'r, you have to stop work for the day, something has happened in the village! Uncle Gimpy hanged himself!

Everyone heard. On that patch of stone, all the cripples stood up, stunned, motionless on that patch of stone. The sun still enflamed that wild hair.

This time someone really did die! This time someone really was sacrificed! Heavens, what did Uncle Gimpy do?

Tianzhu continued shouting, Stop work, go back to the village, something's happened, Uncle Gimpy hanged himself!

Someone said, Impossible, he was at last night's meeting.

Tianzhu was panting like an ox. He said, I already sent two of my kids to Nanliu Village to fetch Uncle Chuandeng. Hurry!

From behind, I saw that head of flame tremble. I heard it say, I never saw that the class struggle in our village was so complicated.

Could anyone have foreseen a hanging? Heavens!

32

Then I saw his eyes.

I finally saw them, a bunch of people gathered on that patch of stone. I shouted, Kugen'r, Kugen'r, you have to stop work for the day, something has happened in the village! Uncle Gimpy hanged himself! All those lowered heads suddenly looked up under the sun, everyone with their mouth and eyes wide open, like a bunch of clay figures thrust up out of the earth. I shouted again, Stop work, go back to the village, something has happened, Uncle Gimpy hanged himself!

Humi said, Impossible, he was perfectly fine at last night's meeting.

Then I saw his eyes. I said, I already sent two of my kids to Nanliu Village to fetch Uncle Chuandeng. Hurry! Can't you see this is fucking important? Is this for real? If it's not for real, who's going to lie in the coffin Uncle Chuandeng is going to build? You? Are you going to fucking lie in it, Humi?

Humi lowered his head and said, You're so crude, swearing at folks. What did I ever do to you to make you hate me so much?

I said, Humi, if someone didn't fucking swear at you every three days, you'd do nothing but spout nonsense. How can someone dead not be real?

Humi said, What did I ever do to you to make you hate me so much?

Then I saw his eyes. It was as if the matter had suddenly confused and frightened him. He was leaning on the bloody red handle of a sledge. His eyes looked like they were filled with lead, heavy and turbid, motionless. I stared at his eyes. *The two of us went to see him this morning; we went, and he hanged himself. Tell me. What is this? If he didn't hang himself on account of us, then why did he do it? No one else knew about us. Tell me. If it wasn't on account of us, then who? Tell me. Is this what's called handling matters? Tell me. That's just great, the fox hasn't been caught and a life has been forfeited. Tell me.*

Those two eyes of his were as emotionless as two stone beads. He was completely oblivious to what I was asking him with my eyes. He was leaning on that sledge handle, shaking his head. He said, I never saw that the class struggle in our village was so complicated.

Fuck it all to hell. Not complicated? The guy just hanged himself! Tell me! Tell us to "never be careless," "never be careless," and still be careless. That's just great. This fucking time there's no need to sweep, to sweep clean—the guy is fucking dead, for fuck's sake! How are we going to handle this?

Those two eyes of his were completely oblivious to what I was asking with my eyes. He said, I never saw that the class struggle in our village was so complicated, too complicated! As he spoke, he reached into his pocket for a handful of fried beans, which he tossed into his mouth and began to chew. Crunching noisily, he looked like a horse.

I saw his eyes and knew that I couldn't count on him. This trouble was mine alone. I said, Humi, you take over Uncle Gimpy's duties tonight—sleep in the stable and feed the donkeys.

Head down, Humi said, I'm not going. I'm scared.

I said, What the fuck are you scared of? A bachelor like you has nothing to worry about. What are you afraid of?

Humi said, If I had a wife, it'd be okay—with a partner, there's nothing to fear. Besides, aren't Tiecheng, Sanguai, and Laofan all poor unmarried guys? Why does it have to be me?

I said, Are you saying that as production team leader, I can't order you? Do you fucking want to overturn the heavens? If you don't fucking go, you needn't ever work for the production team again, or earn work points!

Humi said, If I obey and go, isn't that enough? Won't I starve without work points? I don't know what I owe you that makes you hate me so much.

I said, So what are you standing around for? Get going! When we get back we still have to kill two goats, prepare two meals for Uncle Chuandeng and his assistant, dig a grave for Uncle Gimpy—what a pain in the ass!

I woke that bunch of clay figures. After half of them left, I stopped him and said, Kugen'r, what are we going to do now that things have blown up like this?

He said, Tianzhu, I know what to do. I think that the more complicated class struggle becomes, the firmer we must be in our stand, the more determined we must be to see the struggle through to the end. I have to do this; I just need to try to figure out how to make the best use of it.

I knew he was completely oblivious to what I was asking with my eyes. I didn't intend to say any more to him. When someone in your own village dies, what is there to say to an outsider? If you can't take care of your own affairs, why worry outsiders? Isn't it a waste of time to count on your sister-in-law to raise your son?

Tiecheng turned and asked, Tianzhu, where are we supposed to dig a grave for Uncle Gimpy and bury him?

I said, Do you have to ask? When he was alive, Uncle Gimpy hoed down at Fifteen Mu. He always said that when he died, he wanted to be buried there. Fifteen Mu originally belonged to the Cao family. Nothing ever went right for him in this motherfucking life; what are you going to say when a person dies? Let him be happy this once, let things work out this once, and let him keep watch over Fifteen Mu.

He turned toward me, those beady eyes of his on me, and said, Tianzhu, that won't do. You can't bury a rich peasant on his own land. It's a political issue, this has grave political implications.

I knew he was completely oblivious to what I was asking with my eyes. I said, Everyone stay where you are. We are also democratic, and the important labor force of Stunted Flats is all here. Speak up, everyone: is it okay to bury Uncle Gimpy at Fifteen Mu? Those who agree, raise your hand!

The group of men, who had started to wander off like a bunch of goats on the slopes, looked back, staring blankly at me, without moving. I pressed them, Raise your damned hands!

They all raised their hands but him. About ten black arms shone in the barren land.

I said, Fine, the minority will obey the majority. Fifteen Mu it is.

He stared at me with those eyes of his. It was a waste of time. He was completely oblivious to what I was asking with my eyes.

He said, Tianzhu, I'll go to the stable tonight. In the future, I'll feed the donkeys; there's no need to send anyone else, nor do you need to record the work points for me. I'm just one person, and I can do a little more work for the production team.

I said, Haven't I already assigned Humi?

He said, No need. I hope no one will engage in any superstitious feudal activities on account of this matter! So saying, he pulled out a handful of fried beans.

I didn't reply. It would have been a waste of time. Anyway, he wouldn't listen or see anything but those few things he always talks about, or his fried beans. A person has to handle their own affairs, and I damn well wouldn't count on anyone else.

33

I say "impossible" and he fucking tells me to go lay myself out in the coffin. *To what do I owe your hating me so much? Besides, can you blame me for that? I walked in front, carrying a sack; I don't know where she came from, but she ended up following me. If she hadn't been wa-wa-ing, I never would have seen her. I was walking ahead and she was behind me going Wa-wa. I thought that if I headed into the woods, she'd be afraid to follow. Who could have foreseen that she was so determined to follow me? Who could have seen that by coincidence I was carrying a sack? If you spread a sack on the ground, isn't it the same as mattress? You can't blame me that a sack can motherfucking be used as a mattress, can you? You can't blame me because she was determined to follow me, can you? I know why you hate me. Can you blame me that she kept following me, wa-wa-ing? I went into the woods to gather acorns—I was carrying the sack to gather acorns. But you blame me for spreading the sack on the ground like a mattress and not using it to gather acorns, don't you? The deeper into the woods we went, the denser it got. There were just*

the two of us out there. Why did you marry such a dumb and mute
woman? Like you, I couldn't control myself. You couldn't control
yourself; could I? Besides, she's dumb and mute. Fine, you say she's a
woman or a female animal. If she's a female animal, it's okay for you
to use her, but not me? But you blame me for spreading the sack on
the ground like a mattress and not using it to gather acorns, don't
you? There was no one else there but the two of us. A man and a
woman, a male and a female, can you blame me? Deep in the woods,
I stood there and she kept wa-wa-ing. I said, Don't wa-wa, come
over here. She came over. Tell me, could I control myself? The tree
leaves rustled hua-la, hua-la; *all around, it was nothing but* hua-la,
hua-la, *till you couldn't hear anything else.* Hua-la, hua-la, hua-la,
hua-la *filled the sky and filled the ground. She just kept going Wa-*
wa-wa-wa-wa-wa. I said, My ancestors, my living ancestors, my
damned ancestors! She just went on wa-wa-wa-ing. I know why you
hate me; can you blame me? She just went on wa-wa-wa-ing. The
villagers all say that there is a Humi among the four dogs, and that
it's Third Dog. Why wouldn't I be sure of it? I'd really like to take
Third Dog away. Would that be okay? She just went on wa-wa-wa-
ing. How do I know Third Dog is mine? I say he's mine. Are you okay
with that or not? You won't admit it, so what do you hate me for? I
may have done you wrong, but does that give you the right to tell me
to lay myself out in a coffin? Does your telling me to go lay myself out
in a coffin change anything? Third Dog's father is still his father—if
it's me, nothing changes. Telling me to go lay myself out in a coffin
doesn't make Third Dog any more your son if he's not. What's the
point in hating me? How was I to know she'd want to do it with me?
How was I supposed to know that a sack spread on the ground was
softer than a mattress? How was I to know the leaves were so deep?
How was I to know that there was nothing but hua-la, hua-la? *My*

ancestors, my living ancestors, my damned ancestors! She just kept going Wa-wa-wa. When my mother had me, the rice was in the middle of cooking; by the time I was born, the rice was burnt. So I'm called Humi, or "burnt rice." Third Dog shouldn't be called Third Dog; Third Dog ought to be called Sack, for if I hadn't had that sack, there'd be no Third Dog! Sack, Sack, my son, when will you be able to stand in front of others and simply call me Dad? If you fathered him, you are his father; if you didn't father him, you are not. Yes is yes. No matter what. No is no, no matter what. Third Dog is not Sack. Sack is Third Dog. Sack, my son, do you or don't you know?

I know why you hate me. You hate me on account of Sack. Just because Sack looks like Humi. If Sack didn't look like Humi, who'd he look like? Sack is Humi, Humi is Sack. Hate or no hate, it's all the same. Laid out in a coffin or not laid out in a coffin, it's all the same. It's a sack full of burnt rice; all your fucking hate is for nothing! Without turning around I can see his burning eyes. As soon as he lays eyes on me, his eyes burn. *Burn, go ahead and burn*—I can't do anything about it, I can't tell him to stop. My living ancestors, one day I want to walk up to him and look him straight in those burning eyes and tell him, Third Dog is not called Third Dog, his name is Sack. When Sack was born all the tree leaves were rustling, *hua-la, hua-la, hua-la* filled the sky and the ground. I'll tell him that. *And then it'll be all right if you tell me to go lie in a coffin or hang myself or work my whole life without getting work points or go hungry my whole life!*

I know why he hates me so much. He hates me because Third Dog is not Third Dog, Third Dog is Sack! Just because the sack is filled with burnt rice! Hate or no hate, it's all the same. This whole damned thing was predestined and can't be changed, even by the Old Man in Heaven himself, damn it! Hate or no hate, it's all the same. Sack is Humi. Humi is Sack. *You can't blame me because she always follows you. You can't blame me because a sack spread on the ground became a mattress. You can't blame me that only a man and a woman were out there alone. Hate or no hate, it's all the same.*

34

He finally stopped talking to Ugly Baby and, leaning on that sledge handle reddened with his own blood, turned away. The half-exposed rock embankment full of white uneven hammer blows was like a fresh scar sadly running through the middle of the valley. A slight breeze mussed his hair. The broken skin of his hand hurt the same as if it had been burned by flames. That frequent thought crossed his mind once again. Kugen'r thought, *How can they understand me? I'm the son of a martyr; I am my father; I am changing the world for my father. How can they understand me? A person who so desperately hopes to be understood by others is a weakling. Zhao Yingjie's solitary, steadfast determination to press ahead stemmed from his iron will, not from the understanding of others.*

The early winter sun was like a woman who had just become a grandmother, kindly and warmly placing the mountains and the people at her feet, gently reaching out and caressing the withered brambles on the bleak mountaintops and the hair on people's heads mussed by the wind, gently embracing the frustration that rose like a blurred mountain mist in Kugen'r's heart.

Beside him was a group of laboring men, constantly striking the blasted rock with resonant blows from their tools. Each resonant blow was like a cold, hard pebble, thrown one after another into that sense of frustration, only making it appear deeper and broader. When the green disappeared on the leafless high plains, the only thing that remained was pure distance and pure and simple grayish yellow. Of the four seasons, Kugen'r felt he belonged to the plains in winter; standing amid the grayish yellow immensity, he was deeply moved by his own inexpressible frustration and couldn't help but feel he had gained a solitary vantage point above the world. An inexhaustible and tender regard welled up in his eyes; he projected his frustration and solitude over the speechless mountains, which in turn gave rise to more inexhaustible frustration and solitude. The resonant blows stirred them like a cold wind shaking the last dry leaves on the branch tips of the trees, patiently waiting for them to fall, waiting for them to provide the final explanatory note on the immense plain with their fall. Everything would end in a huge snowfall, end with hill and dale covered in white.

Every winter for the last six years, Kugen'r had had to visit these deep mountain ravines and stand before the rocks. It had already become an unbreakable commandment. The way Kugen'r saw it, of the twelve big and small valleys of Stunted Flats, they could on average remake a valley every two years by blasting the stone. It would take twenty-four years to complete his plan.

The entire male labor force, old and young, of Stunted Flats together consisted of only about thirteen people, all of whom were crippled, with him the only exception. Therefore he had to shoulder the responsibility for the heaviest and most dangerous tasks, such as drilling the rock and setting the explosive charges. Kugen'r perfectly understood that the twenty-four years needed to transform the mountain rivers had, in fact, actually become his personal plan, a test of his determination and will. To face or avoid these rocks had simply become the point of his existence. From time immemorial, no one knows how long the mountains of Stunted Flats had lain there silently, but this was the first time in millions of years that, due to his existence, because he faced them, these rocks and yellow earth possessed real signifi- cance. Every winter, the men laboriously piled up stone em- bankments; by summer, most had been knocked down by flood- waters. But with the arrival of winter, Kugen'r would, as always, take his team to the mountain valleys. This had become a test of iron will between man and mountain. Kugen'r knew there was no retreat and no stopping for him, for stopping would imply that the last six years of striving were a total loss and, even more, that he was totally useless, that he was as meaningless as the yellow earth and stones. While providing him with a throne from which he could look down upon the world, the high plains had also laid an unfathomable trap for him. It was an abyss that could never be filled by time or history.

In this test of will, the only thing that disturbed Kugen'r was the constant hunger. The excessively heavy labor during cold weather only increased his appetite. Regardless of how much he ate, he was always hungry. Hunger was often like a flood inun- dating a sandy beach, and it welled up out of his very flesh and bone. He had no choice but to put down whatever tool he was using when the uncontrollable shaking began. Without reason or mercy, hunger never shrank from reminding Kugen'r of life's existence and its mortal weaknesses. To conquer his hunger,

Kugen'r utilized a method of the people of his hometown, carrying beans and corn cooked in sand in his pockets. The moment he felt hungry, he'd shove handful after handful of the scorched yellow ammunition into his mouth. He would vigorous and noisily chew it up until the corn or beans became a sweet and aromatic liquid between his tongue and teeth, in order to replenish his exhausted will and strength. Whenever he reached that point, the movement of his jaw would remind him more of a horse than a man.

When he turned to face Tianzhu, who was panting, he was assailed by a violent hunger, like a landslide in his innards. He couldn't be sure if it was the news that Uncle Gimpy had hanged himself or hunger that made everything in front of him go blank. He distinctly felt his forehead break out in a sweat. He hurriedly grabbed a handful of fried beans and stuffed them, along with the news that Uncle Gimpy had hanged himself, into his empty belly.

Tianzhu said, You have to stop work, something has happened in the village, Uncle Gimpy hanged himself.

Kugen'r said, I never thought the class struggle in our village was so complicated.

When he said this, his mouth was full of chewed-up beans, filled with the aroma of fried beans. Kugen'r couldn't figure out why Uncle Gimpy would hang himself. Everything had been conducted according to Party policy; everything had just begun. This sudden occurrence turned the struggle that had just begun into an unpredictable kaleidoscope. Uncle Gimpy, the rich peasant, wasn't the only thing hanged from that beam. The imagined results of the class struggle had been completely turned upside down in that room with its horsey odor, even before it started, and been hanged for nothing on that dirty beam.

Kugen'r had some difficulty overcoming the suddenness of the news, much like recovering from a sudden bout of hunger, making him momentarily indecisive. Amid the broken stone stood the half-piled embankment full of gray chip marks, like a freshly opened wound in the mountainous wilds, an ugly sight in the grayish yellow valley. The cold white stream water flowed through the cracks in the stone, then silently and coldly away.

Kugen'r said, I never really thought the class struggle in our village was so complicated, so complicated.

The winter sun hung high and white above the heads of the group of male laborers.

35

That half-built stone embankment was lying there, clear to the eye when you turned to look. Everyone had left. Some had gone up the slope, others had not. Seeing no one around, I called out to stop him.

I said, Humi, have you been sworn at again?

He just laughed and walked around the bend with me. He laughed and said, Anyone who wants to scold a ragged old commune member can damn well do it.

I said, Humi, why doesn't anyone scold me? What the fuck do you owe to him? What wrong did you do to him?

He just laughed again and stopped. He laughed and said, I owe him a dog, but there's nothing to be done about it. Just because I owe him a dog, does that mean he has to swear?

I said, Why didn't you say that to Tianzhu's face?

He just laughed.

I said, You just laugh and don't say anything.

He laughed and said, If I said anything, it wouldn't be Uncle Gimpy hanging there now.

At the mention of Uncle Gimpy, we fell silent. All that could be heard was the sound of footsteps. That half-built stone embankment lay at the bottom of the valley, motionless, clear to the eye when you turned back to look. The group of men shuffled away from there on their way back to the village.

I said, Humi, what's the meaning of spending a whole life shuffling back and forth?

He smiled and said, Ugly Baby, you can't ask me that—you have to ask someone who has already reached the end.

I said, Who's reached the end?

He said, Uncle Gimpy.

I said, Nonsense. How can you ask a dead guy?

He smiled and said, In this life, no living person has reached the end yet. If you haven't reached the end yet, how can you know the purpose? Whereas the dead have all reached the end. Only when you reach the end will you know the purpose. But there's no point in knowing, because you can't tell anyone. No matter how hard you try, you'll never find out. Uncle Gimpy has reached the end, but who can find out what he's doing?

I said, What was it with Uncle Gimpy? Why did he do it?

He said, Uncle Gimpy was a fool. He just wanted to jump the gun on the Old Man in Heaven. Actually, it doesn't matter what a person does in life, it doesn't matter if they enjoy life or suffer; in the end, the Old Man in Heaven gives you only one road—everyone dies in the end. Willing, you have to die; unwilling, you still have to die. Uncle Gimpy jumped the gun on the Old Man in Heaven. Why jump the gun? If it's yours, it's yours. If it's not yours, it's not yours. If it's not yours, even if you snatch it, it's still not yours. If you don't snatch it and it's yours, it's still yours. Uncle Gimpy didn't do anything in life save feed a few donkeys, nothing else. So what was there to jump the gun for? In a hurry, you have to die; not in a hurry, you still have to die. Anyway, it's death. It's that one road. Willing, you have to take it; unwilling, you still have to take it. There's no other road you can take. You say he was in a hurry? Uncle Gimpy was a fool.

I swore at him. I said, What the fuck are you talking about? Circle around and circle back, like a donkey on a millstone path.

He said, It's worse than a donkey on a millstone path. In life, a man is never unhitched from his millstone. Pulling it around and around, he can no longer pull before he's old, so he has a little one. Born to pull, it pulls and bears. It goes on and on without end. Besides those donkeys, Uncle Gimpy didn't have a wife or child, so why jump the gun?

I said, Just like a poor unmarried guy—you can't stop talking about a wife and children.

He said, Of course. If Uncle Gimpy had a wife and kids, do you think he would have hanged himself? I'd like to have a wife. If I had a wife, I wouldn't beat her or scold her; if we had something good to eat, I'd let her eat first; if we had new clothes, she'd be the first to wear them. I'd want to have a pile of kids with her and raise them and then watch as our kids had kids of their own. I don't think there is anything better or more beautiful under Heaven than that.

I just smiled. I said, You're no better than others. Your wife and kids run on the millstone path of others. You've got no one to run for you on the fucking millstone path, but you've got a son who blindly runs on someone else's millstone path.

He smiled. He laughed and said, Sack! Sack!

I swore at him again. You've fucking gone crazy thinking about a wife. More nonsense!

He smiled. He laughed.

That half-built stone embankment lay at the bottom of the valley, deep and far away. Looking back, you could see it. The newly broken stone shone white under the sun, dazzling white. It stopped a stream of cold, bright mountain water, which poured through the cracks in the stone, flowing away, cold and bright. A group of men had shuffled past here, and must have shuffled back again to the village.

Tianzhu suddenly sang out loudly, making his face turn red and veins pop out on his neck.

That half-built stone embankment lay motionless on the valley floor. The newly broken and exposed stone was white. From a distance it looked like a motionless corpse laid out in the valley.

And you ask why Uncle Gimpy did it?

36

Fuck it all to hell! Live as a fool! Die as a fool!

Xue Meng weeps at once.
Turning his head to look back at the world,

He sees not one bit of it;

He doesn't see his little brother in Wuying.

Striking my horse, I pass through the willow grove.

Seeing Xue Gang, I tremble with rage.

Live as a fool! Die as a fool! Fuck it all to hell!

37

Uncle Chuandeng Uncle Chuandeng Uncle Chuandeng my dad wants you and Erniu to hurry over and make a coffin for Uncle Gimpy we didn't see anything we just ate a handful of beans there was a rope above Uncle Gimpy's head Commune Head Liu cut him down with an axe everyone in the village saw it he cut him down when he cut down Uncle Gimpy then he fell hurry up my dad is waiting for you at the village we still have to buy cigarettes my dad said if we're short one *fen* he'll beat the hell out of us

38

They made me fast the green one inside the green one inside the green one is silent the green one doesn't pay attention to me inside they made me fast the green one pays no attention to me they made me fast

39

I knew he was unwilling. But I'm the leader. *Do you know what a leader is? To be a leader means that you must lead when you are willing and you must also lead when you are unwilling. Willing or unwilling, you must lead!*

I said, Okay, we'll see; that's the way it was at the scene. It was suicide. There's no need to look into it. Go with me to the cave. I've got an assignment for you.

He lifted his eyes to look at me. He didn't move. I knew he was unwilling. But I'm the leader.

I said, Let's go, Kugen'r. I still have to visit other production teams to pass on the central Party documents, after which I'll go back to the commune. I must speak with you before I leave. I have an assignment for you.

He walked behind me. I knew he was unwilling. But I'm the leader!

Back at the cave, I said, Kugen'r, take out your notebooks. You must record the work assigned by the leader.

Looking at me, he took out his notebooks. I knew he was unwilling.

I said, There are three things: first, the rich peasant Cao Yongfu, fearing punishment for his crimes, committed suicide, fully demonstrating the sharp nature and complexity of the class conflict at Stunted Flats. Second, the incident must be used to stir up a high tide of mass criticism, and each and every one of his crimes must be brought to light and thoroughly criticized. Third, write up the facts of the incident and report them to the commune to bring it to the attention of the other production teams and units.

In silence he recorded each item. I knew he was unwilling.

I said, Kugen'r, this issue is still an issue. If every damned teacher by negative example died and only us positive people were left, there wouldn't be much of a class struggle left to wage and all future political movements would be difficult to carry out.

He looked at me and said, I really never thought the class struggle of Stunted Flats was so complicated. It never entered my mind.

He just looked at me. I knew what he was thinking. I knew what he was thinking in his heart. *No matter how complicated this matter is, do you think you can just put this on the leader? By making it more complicated? Do you think you're something special because you have more education than I do? You think it's fine, that you can do anything you want? You might know more words than I do, but have you faced the number of bullets I have? When I was engaged in the revolution, bullets flew everywhere. Are you aware of that? Where were you when Political Commissar Wang fell into my arms? Where were you when I swore my oath to Political Commissar Wang? I told him I would spend my whole life here watching over him. Do you think this can be done by simply reciting a few lines from the quotations of Chairman Mao?*

He said, Commune Head Liu, don't worry. We want to see the class struggle in Stunted Flats through to the end! We will not rest until victory is ours!

I knew he was unwilling; I knew what he was thinking. *But can you conduct this against your leaders? I spent my whole life working here. How many days have you been here? Do you think you can do anything you want because you know a few more words than I do?*

Patting him on the shoulder, I said, Kugen'r, work hard. This is an opportunity for you to steel and temper yourself. Work hard when the leaders are around, and work just as hard when they are not. I have to go back to the commune. Walk with me a ways, I want to speak with you.

He just followed behind me. When we got to the earthen cliff at the entrance to the village, he stopped. He raised his eyes and looked at me. I knew what he wanted to say. I took out those blank letters of introduction and handed them to him.

I said, Kugen'r, these blank letters of introduction are not to be taken lightly—they represent the Commune Party Committee's trust in you, the power given to you by the Party. You are the orphan son of a martyr, and the Party must rely on people like you to take over the work.

He didn't say anything. He raised his eyes and looked up at me. I knew what he wanted to say.

I said, You're not called Kugen'r; your name is Zhao Weiguo, Comrade Zhao Weiguo. The great enterprise of purifying class ranks in Stunted Flats is entirely up to you. If in the future you need a transfer, just go to the County Party Office and do the paperwork, and these pieces of paper will come in handy. If you have any other difficulties, do not hesitate to make things known to the commune. The Commune Party Committee knows that you have applied for Party membership. Work hard, achieve something amid these great storms, and I'll sponsor you.

Still he remained silent. I knew what he was thinking. *You think I don't dare say what's on my mind? If I don't dare speak my mind on my own turf, who will? Say something, open your mouth—I want to see what you're capable of.*

I said, Kugen'r, you're still young; you've never been married, so you don't know how miserable it is without a woman. Nuanyu's place is neat and tidy, and she's a good cook. In this poverty-stricken place of ours, when the work of the revolution is accomplished, there'll be nothing left to do, nothing for amusement. I came to Stunted Flats to work in the countryside and whenever I return, I stay at Nuanyu's. She has a two-room cave—she lives in one room and I stay in the other. Okay, there's no need to stare at me, just purify the class ranks.

I finished speaking and left. *I really want to see what you are capable of! I want to see what you can do to me! Chairman Mao says, "The force at the core leading our cause forward is the Chinese Communist Party." Do you know who the force at the core of running the Yellow Earth People's Commune is? Damn it, it's me!*

40

He dragged along behind me, but I ignored him. I inhaled deeply. Before I entered through the door, I could already smell that heady aroma. I inhaled deeply again. So fragrant, it smelled so good—the smell of candy, tobacco, wine, coal oil, cookies, and hemp rope all mixed together. I never smelled anything so good at home. When I stood on my tiptoes and lifted the money above my head, all I saw was that mouthful of big yellow teeth. He dragged along behind me, but I ignored him.

I stood on my tiptoes and pressed against the counter. Everything was so bright and colorful. I inhaled deeply, lifted the money above my head, and saw that mouthful of big yellow teeth.

I said, I want to buy a carton of Greenleaf cigarettes. One forty. Here's two *yuan*, you've got to give me six *mao* in change, not one *fen* less. My dad said if I'm short, he'll beat the hell out of me.

Big Yellowteeth smiled. Big Yellowteeth didn't take my money; he looked down and said, Which village?

I said, Stunted Flats.

Big Yellowteeth said, Which family?

I said, Tianzhu is my dad.

Big Yellowteeth smiled again and said, Oh, you're two of the idiot's kids.

Lifting the money above my head, I said, I want to buy a carton of Greenleaf cigarettes.

Still smiling, Big Yellowteeth said, Can't be short? I guess the idiot's kid isn't an idiot too, is he?

I said, I want to buy a carton of Greenleaf cigarettes.

Fucking Big Yellowteeth! My brother dragged along behind me, but I ignored him. He said, Brother, I want a piece of candy, I want a piece of candy. I turned around and gave him a shove and swore, Why are you such a fucking pest? I jerked him toward me and said, Second Dog, we're not getting any candy. Everything smells so good here, smell, take a deep breath! Rubbing his face, he began to cry, Brother, I want a piece of candy.

Big Yellowteeth smiled and said, You'd dare to eat a piece of candy? If you're short, your dad will beat the hell out of you.

You'd dare to eat a piece of candy? Hurry on home with your brother.

¹ That fucking Big Yellowteeth!

Big Yellowteeth handed me the cigarettes as he spoke. I took the cigarettes and the change. I counted it—six *mao*. That fucking Big Yellowteeth. I took out one bill and lifted it in front of his face.

I said, I want one *mao*'s worth of candy.

Big Yellowteeth said, Really? If you're short one *mao*, won't your dad beat the hell out of you?

I said, I want one *mao*'s worth of candy.

Big Yellowteeth said, Are you sure?

I said, I want one *mao*'s worth of candy!

Big Yellowteeth grabbed a handful of candy and said, Two *fen* apiece, five pieces for one *mao*.

I took the candy and counted it—five pieces. That fucking Big Yellowteeth. I handed it to Second Dog and said, Here, eat up.

Second Dog finally smiled. Second Dog stuck a piece of candy in his mouth. Second Dog said, Brother, it's sweet.

I scolded him, What do you mean, sweet? You didn't even take the wrapper off of it!

Second Dog spit out the candy, unwrapped it, and stuck it back in his mouth. Second Dog said, Brother, it really is sweet! Second Dog handed me a piece and said, Here, you try one too.

I said, You eat it. I don't want any. That fucking Big Yellowteeth. I said, Second Dog, hurry up, Uncle Gimpy's waiting for the cigarettes so that things can get done.

Coming out the door, Second Dog said, Brother, what are we going to do if Dad beats us?

I said, Don't worry, it's just some candy.

Second Dog said, Dad's going to beat us.

I said, Don't worry, I'll just tell him I lost a *mao*.

Second Dog took another piece of candy and said, Brother, you have one too.

I took it and stuck it in my mouth. Fuck, it really was sweet!

I said, Second Dog, remember, Big Yellowteeth is a jerk. When we grow up and have money, we won't buy his stuff, not even one *fen*'s worth.

Second Dog said, Okay, Brother. Brother, it's really sweet.

I said, Second Dog, remember that all adults are bad. When we grow up let's not be bad, we'll be good to piss them off.

Second Dog said, Okay, Brother. But we're all cripples and won't grow up. Brother, it's really sweet!

41

There's a lantern hanging on the left column. There's a lantern hanging on the right column. Two lanterns to illuminate the stage at the Earth God's temple. Today is the last performance of Little Five. The two lanterns make the freshly cut poplar coffin boards look so white. Little Five is still lying in the stable, waiting for me to make this coffin for him. When I came, I knew I'd be up all night, so I had Erniu bring the lanterns along. There's one lantern hanging on the left column, there's one lantern hanging on the right column. Two lanterns hanging there to illuminate the last performance of Little Five. You have to listen if you want to; you still have to listen even if you don't want to. *Little Five, why were you in such a hurry? Were you afraid that you'd die after me and not be able to lie in one of my coffins? You're twenty years younger than me. Why were you in such a hurry?* First the big saw, then the little saw, then the adze, then the plane, then the auger, then the axe. You have to listen if you want to; you still have to listen even if you don't want to. Two lanterns hanging there to illuminate the last performance of Little Five. Tianzhu asked me where I wanted to work. Need he ask? Who wants to have a coffin in their courtyard? Where else but here at the temple? I've done two things in this life—build houses for the living and build coffins for the dead. I've done it my whole life. *Why were you in such a hurry?*

Erniu! The line! Watch the black line! If you don't use your eyes, what sort of crooked mess will you end up with? Are you fucking sawing your way back to Nanliu Village? Are you sawing boards or swaying to the rice sprout song? Can't you see with two lanterns hanging there? Are you blind?

If you tell them, they don't get it; if you don't tell them, they still don't get it. Do they have a clue as to what a coffin is? Is a coffin just a couple of poplar-wood boards with a top nailed on? They've never seen the likes of that coffin I made. The coffin I built for the Second Grandma of the Di family, now that was a real coffin. Clear cypress wood, three *cun* thick; I made it wide at the head and narrow at the foot. It was so shiny I didn't need to lacquer it. Before I nailed on the lid, I peeped inside at her. Her face was powdered, her eyebrows painted, and she was dressed entirely in red silk embroidered with auspicious Buddhist symbols.

She wore gold earrings, gold bracelets, and a pair of embroidered shoes for her bound feet. It was as if a living actress from the stage had been placed in the coffin. She had led a comfortable and boring life, and ended her days by swallowing opium. *What do you have? Nothing but a few poplar-wood planks. So why were you in such a hurry?*

Erniu! The line! Watch the line! If your hand is off by one *cun*, the board will be cut crooked by a *cun*. Did I waste my time teaching you? Did you forget? I'm going to chop off that hand of yours!

The glue pot is on the fire. Smoke is spurting out from under the lid, one ring after another spins over the stage, as if they must separate the stage from the night sky or as if they were afraid of the night sky rushing in. A lantern on the left, a lantern on the right, two lanterns make Little Five's coffin shine so bright. I have to boil the glue thoroughly. I have to firmly seal the boards and nail them tightly together. It has to be buried in the ground for ten or twenty years without cracking, the glue splitting, or the joints separating. No cracks, splits, or separations make a coffin? Made even better, it's still a coffin. Everyone is the same—sooner or later we all lie down in a coffin. I've built them my whole life. *Why were you in such a hurry?*

Erniu! Sharpen your saw. Can't you hear the sound it's making? You simpleton, don't you find it hard going? Even a donkey knows how to pull a light cart. You're worse than a fucking donkey! Fetch the file.

Oh, everyone's in a hurry, everyone. In a hurry to be born, in a hurry to die. In a hurry to move into a house, in a hurry to lie down in a coffin. In a hurry to chop down trees. It's as if everyone were born afraid to let something slip by. But the Old Man in Heaven has already arranged things. For every living person, there is a tree. If you live eight years, that's a tree. If you live eighty years, that's a tree. Everything is arranged by the Old Man in Heaven. Oh, everything is chopped down. It's nothing but *chop, chop*. No one thinks about it, but if everything is chopped down, then what? It's just *chop, chop*. A mountain, a mountain is clear cut and all that's left is people, a mountain full of people. Only when the people fall do you think about the trees. You want to snatch something from the Old Man in Heaven, but there's nothing left. Where do you go to search? Now a tree is scarcer than ginseng. Everything's gone. What's left to snatch? Nothing. *Why the big hurry? Are you snatching something from the Old Man in Heaven? Or from yourself?*

Erniu! Oil the saw! Saw with skill. The oilcan is in the pack. Go get it.

There's a lantern hung on the east column, there's a lantern hung on the west column. Two lanterns clearly illuminate Little Five's last performance. Two lanterns make the coffin boards shine white. Dazzling white. There's nothing but these few coffin boards. There's a fire, and on the fire is the glue pot. Smoke is spurting out from under the lid, one ring after another spins on the stage, as if they must separate the stage from the night sky or as if they were afraid of the night sky rushing in. Second Grandma has gold earrings, gold bracelets, and clothes covered with auspicious Buddhist symbols. She also had opium. *What did you have, Little Five? You had nothing but a few donkeys to feed for the team and these few coffin boards.*

Erniu! Add some oil, saw with skill. A little more oil.

Two lanterns illuminate Little Five's last performance. There's nothing on the stage save a few coffin boards. *If it weren't for Tianzhu, you wouldn't even have these few poplar boards. You're twenty years younger than me! Little Five, why were you in such a hurry? Keeping me and Erniu up all night for you. There's nothing to your final performance save these few poplar coffin boards.*

42

I never worked on a stage. I never made a coffin on stage. That's what she said, she said I look like her brother. How could you two be so alike! She was bundled up in that quilted print jacket, red, tight, like that painting of Li Tiemei. That's what she said. I just ate. I never ate such tasty dumplings. Once the two oil lanterns were hung, the stage was very bright, making these few poplar coffin boards of Uncle Gimpy's shine ever so white. I just saw, *chi-la, chi-la, chi-la*. I never worked on a stage. I never made a coffin on stage.

My master just swore at me, Erniu! The line! Watch the line, or everything will end up crooked and such. Are you fucking sawing your way back to Nanliu Village? I told you to saw the boards. Did I tell you to sway to a rice sprout song? Can't you see with two lanterns hanging there? Are you blind?

I sat with my master on the *kang* in the cave. My master sat at the head, I sat to the side. She brought a huge bowl of mutton dumplings over. She said, Uncle Chuandeng, you two hurry and have some. Then she turned and smiled at me. She was bundled up in a quilted print jacket and looked like Li Tiemei in the painting.

She said, Why do you look so much like my brother? You two look so much alike. Even your names are similar. My brother's name was Huniu and you're called Erniu. Why do you look so much like him? We just butchered the sheep this afternoon, eat up, enjoy.

I just ate. I never ate such tasty dumplings.

Master said, Erniu!

I put down my bowl. I knew my master is going to complain about how noisily I eat, how I wolf down my food.

She smiled. She said, What's wrong? A person should be able to eat any way they want. As long as it tastes good! Eat up, Erniu.

I picked up my bowl again. I ate. I never ate such tasty dumplings.

She said, You even eat the same way. You really look like him. You two really look very much alike!

I ate. My master ate. She didn't eat. After we finished eating, she cleaned up.

Master asked her, Why don't you eat?

She said, The meat and flour all belong to the team. It was prepared to take care of Uncle Gimpy's business. Only those who work are entitled to eat.

Master said, Didn't you make his burial clothes for him?

She said, That wasn't work assigned by the team. I did it on my own.

I said, You're such a nice person, so why do you want to live in this village of cripples?

Master said, Erniu!

She was angry. She didn't lift her head, but I knew she was angry. Head lowered, she scrubbed the pot, scrubbing harder and harder. I don't even use so much force when I cut wood with an axe.

She didn't lift her head to look at me. She said, Aren't Beijing and Taiyuan better than here? Why is it that a good person like you doesn't move to Beijing or Taiyuan? Why live in this poor area of ours?

She had me right away with her question. She left me feeling pretty bad. I couldn't even answer her.

Master said, Erniu, let's go. He's still in the stable waiting for us.

I left with my master. I had no idea why she was so angry. I wouldn't have opened my mouth if I'd known it was going to make her mad.

She said, Uncle Chuandeng, I'm boiling water. I'll bring it to you guys when it's ready.

I quickly said, That's okay, there's no need. I'll come and get it, I'll come and get it.

She still paid no attention to me. I said, I didn't know you'd get angry; otherwise I wouldn't have opened my mouth. Actually, Stunted Flats isn't all that bad. I wouldn't mind living here myself. Really. If I'd known, I wouldn't have opened my mouth.

She smiled and said, Is such a young fellow already capable of such nonsense? If Stunted Flats was such a nice place, it wouldn't be called Stunted Flats. Actually, people are just like trees. A tree has no choice as to where it sprouts and grows—it's fate.

Master called me from the courtyard, Erniu!

She said again, You really look like my brother. I never knew two people could look so much alike!

Master called again, Erniu!

I hurried out into the darkness. She stood in the doorway, the light streaming from behind her. She stood in the light, red and bundled up, like the painting of Li Tiemei.

This was the first time I worked on a stage, and it was the first time I ever built a coffin on a stage. The first time was to build a coffin for Uncle Gimpy. Master kept pressing me, and I worked my ass off with the saw, *chi-la, chi-la, chi-la, chi-la. Why would such a nice person like her want to live in a rotten, sick place like this?*

Master scolded me again, The line! Watch the line! If your hand is off by a *cun*, your sawing will be off by a *cun*. Did I waste my time teaching you? Did you forget? I'll chop off your hands!

I drank two bowls of soup and I'm still thirsty. *I wonder if the water has boiled. Why would such a nice person like her want to live in a rotten, sick place like this? Want to live in Stunted Flats? Uncle Gimpy was born here and grew up here, but why did he do himself in? I wonder if the water has boiled? Why hasn't she come yet?* Bundled up in that quilted cotton print jacket, she looked like that painting of Li Tiemei.

43

I sat on the cattail mat and held a bundle of stalks with my legs and arms, feeding it in little by little. He cut it with a hay cutter, *gecha-gecha-gecha*. The finger-thick millet stalks were cut in lengths crosswise, in cracker-thin disks that fell outside the cutter. His hand was wrapped in a handkerchief and each time he cut, he frowned; cut and frowned, cut and frowned. Drops of sweat dripped from his brow as he cut, cut and dripped, cut and dripped.

I said, Kugen'r, let's change places.

He said, No need. You feed the stalks better than I do.

I said, Look at how you sweat, look at your hand.

He said, Don't worry. Humi, didn't you say one *cun* of stalks takes three cuts, and even the thin ones will fatten up?

I said, Even if it is fatter, it is still a beast. But are we human?

He said, Don't worry—two more bundles will be enough.

I said, Then let's take a rest.

I removed the bundle from the hay cutter. He stood up and lifted his shirt to wipe away his sweat. His face was red and shiny in the light of the lantern. He pulled a handful of fried beans from his pocket and crunched on them noisily, savoring them like a horse. He looked at me, smiled, and said, I'm hungry. He took another handful from his pocket and, handing them to me, said, You want some?

I said, Sure.

I too crunched on them noisily, savoring them like a horse.

Out of the dark came the sound of wood being sawed, *chi-la, chi-la, chi-la.* It was Uncle Chuandeng and Erniu sawing the boards for Uncle Gimpy's coffin. Erhei was still there digging, *dig, thud, dig, thud*; and after enough digging, Erhei brayed, Ee-aw, ee-aw. What's Erhei doing? Does he have a human nature? Does he know that Uncle Gimpy hanged himself? Does he know that Uncle Gimpy is dead? The window is still open like a big black hole. Uncle Gimpy lies in the big black hole without uttering a sound. Uncle Gimpy is dead. Uncle Gimpy hanged himself. Uncle Gimpy can't talk. Uncle Gimpy lies in that big black hole without moving or uttering a sound. He doesn't feel cold or hungry, doesn't know if it's light or dark, or that Uncle Chuandeng is sawing wood for him, that Erhei is digging, thudding, or that Kugen'r and I are cutting millet stalks. Uncle Gimpy can't see, knows nothing, can't say anything—it's all nothing. *Uncle Gimpy, did you want to snatch something from the Old Man in Heaven? Why were you in such a hurry? You didn't snatch anything—everything was arranged by the Old Man in Heaven. You don't have anything, everything was for nothing, so what did you snatch?* If it belongs to you, it's yours. If it doesn't belong to you, even if you snatch it, it's still not yours. Right is right. Wrong is wrong. Wrong is right? Right is wrong? *Chi-la, chi-la, chi-la, chi-la, chi-la.* The sky was as black as the bottom of a pot; the earth was as black as the bottom of a pot. Uncle Chuandeng is sawing, *chi-la, chi-la, chi-la,* as if sawing through the pot from inside. *Why didn't you get here sooner, Uncle Chuandeng? If you had, you could have sawed the black bottom of the pot in half by now, sawed it apart, which would have saved Uncle Gimpy the trouble of hanging himself and me of cutting millet stalks, saved me the trouble of everything.* The way the old folks tell it, back before everything, there was no sky, earth, mountains, forests, people, crops, or beasts; there wasn't a damned thing. There were just two black pots stuck together. Later, a god by the name of Pan Gu woke up, took up an axe, and struck with all his might, separating Heaven and Earth. Starting then, there was sky, earth, mountains, forests, people, crops, and beasts, there was every damned thing. Pan Gu must have been a carpenter; otherwise, where did he get the axe? With one blow, Pan Gu started an unending stream of dynasties, an unending stream of right and wrong, an unending stream of birth and death; created Uncle Gimpy who hanged himself, created Humi and his Sack, created Kugen'r who's working a hay cutter, created Tianzhu who swears every day at Humi, created Erhei who digs, thudding, on and on, never ever ending . . . *chi-la, chi-la, chi-la, chi-la . . . Why didn't you get here sooner, Uncle Chuandeng? If you and Erniu don't have enough energy, I'll help you and we could saw these two pots split apart by Pan Gu in half again, saw them apart! That would bring an end to that unending stream, and everything would be all right.* Erhei brayed, Ee-aw, ee-aw, ee-aw. *Don't cry, Erhei. You can't bring him back by braying. Uncle Gimpy hanged himself, Uncle Gimpy is dead. You cry, but he doesn't know it. You cry, but he doesn't hear it. Uncle Gimpy is dead, and dying means that everything is wrong . . . chi-la, chi-la, chi-la, chi-la, chi-la . . .* over and over again, never ever ending. . . .

He pressed me and said, Humi, let's hurry up and cut this. Erhei is braying because he's so hungry.

The only thing he knows how to do is cut stalks. He doesn't know a motherfucking thing!

I said, Kugen'r, you'd better keep an eye on Erhei tonight. It seems there's something not quite fucking right about him. It's like he knows Uncle Gimpy hanged himself, that Uncle Gimpy is dead!

He said, Humi, Erhei is a donkey. How could a donkey know these things? Don't start in with that feudal superstition.

The only thing he knows how to do is cut stalks. He doesn't know a motherfucking thing.

I said, Kugen'r, you left the city to come out and suffer here in Stunted Flats. What exactly was it you were thinking?

He shook his head and said, If I told you, you wouldn't understand; if I told you, you wouldn't get it. None of you understands what I am trying to do. You'll never understand what I'm trying to do. Let's cut.

The only thing he knows how to do is cut stalks. He doesn't know a damned thing.

The sky was so dark. Uncle Chuandeng was sawing, *chi-la, chi-la, chi-la*. Erhei was digging, thudding, digging, thudding.

I sat down on the cattail mat again, held the bundle with my legs and arms, feeding it in little by little. He cut it with the hay cutter. *Gecha-gecha-gecha.* The finger-thick millet stalks are cut in lengths, in cracker-thin disks that fall outside the cutter. Each time he cut, he frowned; cut and frowned, cut and frowned. Drops of sweat dripped from his brow as he cut, cut and dripped, cut and dripped. *Gecha-gecha-gecha*, over and over again, never ending.

She arrived while we were cutting. She walked toward us with her hand outstretched, going Wa-wa-wa-wa-wa. No one knew what she wanted to do or say.

I said, What are you doing here? Damn it, you don't need to feed the animals.

She just went Wa-wa-wa-wa.

Kugen'r said, Hurry home and eat, Tianzhu is probably worried about you. Go on.

She just went Wa-wa-wa-wa.

I said, What do you want?

She just went Wa-wa-wa-wa.

Erhei was digging, thud, digging, thud, digging, thud, digging, thud. Uncle Chuandeng and Erniu were still there sawing, *chi-la, chi-la, chi-la*. The two of us were still cutting, *gecha-gecha-gecha*. So wrapped up in our work that we didn't know what the other was doing. Over and over again without end. If anyone knew, he would be the carpenter, he would be Pan Gu.

44

The red one the red one the red one the red one stands here the green one the green one the green one the green one is inside the green one doesn't speak the green one pays no attention to me the green one doesn't feed me the green one is inside the green one doesn't feed me

45

Wa-wa-wa ... wu-wa-wa-wa-wa ... ya-wa-wa-wa-wa. . . .

46

Erhei, Erhei, don't dig. Aren't you tired? Why don't you behave and not worry folks? Didn't I get up early and tell you, when you got back from work you wouldn't see me? The one lying in there isn't me. Why don't you understand? Think about it: if that were me, could I ignore you? Wouldn't I feed you? Who do I care for in the world more than you? Why don't you understand? I hanged myself. Hanging is when you tie a rope so tight around yourself that you can't breathe. You can't breathe, so you die. When someone dies it means not being able to talk, to move, to pet you, to feed you, or to care for you. Dead is dead, it's nothing. It means never being able to see, to pet, to get angry, be happy, be sad, be homesick, leave home, return home, love you, cry, laugh, eat, drink; you can't do anything. Erhei, Erhei, why can't you understand? Digging, braying, and crying are all of no use. I can't open my mouth now, you can't hear what I say, and I said what I had to say this morning. Just think about it: if I hadn't said everything and told you how to behave, could I have left you? Erhei, don't dig, bray, or cry. You can't be angry with death, you can't grieve over death, nor cry about death. If you get angry, grieve, or cry about death, it means you won't be able to get by. Erhei, think about it: how could you let death speak to you, let death care for you, or let death feed you? Erhei, don't keep digging and crying. Erhei, lift your head and look at the sky. What does the sky look like right now? What do you see, Erhei? Do you see anything but the black sky and black earth? Do you know how deep that blackness is? How vast? How far it extends? How long? Do you know where that blackness comes from? Where it goes? Do you know when it started? Do you know when it will no longer be? Erhei, don't cry. If you must see me, lift your head and look at the black sky, the black earth. That blackness with no sides, no edge, no head, no tail, no inside, no outside, no top, and no bottom is me. It's you who the lantern illuminates and it's you who is alive. I am death. That lantern is really small. Small enough to make a person worry, feel distressed, and feel afraid. All your lantern has to do is go out in just a moment and life becomes death, becomes nothing, and you become me. *Erhei, you're a wick no larger than a pea, you're just the blink of an eye.* Before you understand, you have nothing, you are nothing. If you're sad or angry again, if you don't know how to care for yourself, you won't even have this wick, this blink of an eye; nothing will remain. By then, regrets will be too late. You won't be in time for regrets. If you want to be regretful, you won't have a time or place to be so. *Erhei, listen to me, don't cry. Don't be angry. Lift your head and look at the sky and look at the earth, and you'll know where I am.* Don't think that black is nothing, the absence of everything. That's what I used to think. I used to think that all you had to do was close your eyes for everything to be black and there was nothing, that it was nothing, equally dark inside and outside of you, equally empty. All you have to do is close your eyes; then all that remains is the black sky and the black earth, with no sides or edges, nothing, isn't, and can't; all that remains can't be changed, filled up, got rid of; nothing, isn't, and can't. Now I know—now that I have stopped breathing and can't move, now that I am really dead, now that I have become this heaven and earth of blackness—what it means to have, to be, and to do. Melting in the blackness, I can now clearly see that lamp with a pea-sized wick. I know how bright that lamp is, how warm, how precious, how loved. *I love you dearly, I really do, I love you so dearly that I feel deep anxiety about you, that it rends heaven and earth, and that it is going to snatch me out of this blackness. Erhei! Erhei! Erhei! Erhei! You can't hear me or see me, but you cannot but know that I dearly love you. Whether I am here or not, alive or not, whether I stand under the sun or in the dark, I dearly love you. You are my Erhei. Erhei, don't be anxious, don't be angry, don't cry, don't bray, don't dig, because you won't touch or see me. But you know that I dearly love you. You are the thing I love most under heaven. I love you so dearly that I feel such a deep anxiety for you that it rends heaven and earth, and it's going to snatch me out of this blackness. Erhei, behave and don't cry, be anxious, or dig. Don't let death get you down, don't get yourself down. You must learn to love yourself. You must learn to let that pea-sized wick in your lamp shine, burn, and give off warmth. As long as it is there, I know you are here, that I am here, and that the feeling in my heart is here. As long as it is there, I know I am here, that you are here, and the feeling in your heart is there. Erhei, lift your head. Erhei, look. Erhei, what do you see? Do you see the black sky and earth? You see that there is nothing, that nothing can be done, that nothing is, right? Erhei? When you see these, you see me, and you see the feeling in my heart. Erhei, look at me, look at the feeling in my heart; then you will see everything. You'll see everything and have no need to look again. Erhei, close your eyes; don't be anxious, don't be angry, and don't cry. Erhei, close your eyes and rest. Behave, Erhei. Close your eyes, Erhei. Are they closed? Close them. Erhei's eyes are closed. Good Erhei. Erhei is a good boy. Erhei . . . Erhei . . . Erhei . . . Erhei . . . Erhei . . . Erhei . . . Erhei . . . Erhei . . . black sky black earth . . . black sky black earth . . . black sky black earth . . . black sky black earth . . . ErheiErheiErheiblackskyblackearthblackskyblackearthblackskyblackearthblackblackblackblackblackblackblackblackblackblackblackblackblackblackblack. . . .*

47

Sitting alone under the cold light of the lamp, Kugen'r thought, *Death is just death, death is the end of life, and nothing else. I am a materialist, and I am not afraid.* Kugen'r has had these thoughts many times. The cold, dim lamplight was like a magnifying class that coldly magnified his thoughts.

That overpowering horsey smell had lost some of its bite. His lantern sat on the windowsill, a book rested on his knees—a book by Chairman Mao. An austere gloominess and the boundless darkness seeped in through the cracks in the window. The lantern flame flickered constantly because there was no lantern glass. In the light of the lantern, his shadow was cast huge and slanted. Whenever the lantern flickered, a massive dark slanted thing shook, surging toward him over the uneven wall. He couldn't help but look up from his book and look at that approaching shadow. The door curtain had been lowered to separate the indoors from outdoors. But it kept swaying, moving each time the wind blew. He knew he wasn't going out, so he finally decided it was best to keep it raised. No sooner was the door curtain lifted than Uncle Gimpy, who was lying there, exhibited half his ashen head and half of his bloated body. The light at dusk enlarged that half body. Kugen'r looked up at the shadow on the wall and then at the corpse on the *kang*. Kugen'r thought, *I am a materialist and I am not afraid*. But Kugen'r felt an inexplicable discomfort rising along his back. It too was coldly magnified by the lantern light. The donkeys beside him ate noisily with relish, *crunch, crunch, crunch*, filling the stable. Only Erhei stood blankly at the far side, without eating or moving. Kugen'r thought, *Am I a little hungry?* This thought was followed with the thought, *No, I just ate.* This in turn was followed by the thought, *But why do I still feel a little hungry?* Kugen'r reached unconsciously into his pocket for a handful of fried beans. When he put the beans in his mouth, he noticed from the corner of his eye that the huge shadow on the wall extended a hand and put something in its mouth. Watching that shadow, Kugen'r lowered his hand. Kugen'r thought, *That's a shadow; a shadow is just a shadow, a shadow is produced by lamplight. The shadow isn't me, it can't eat.* As if to confirm his thoughts, as if to prove his thoughts, Kugen'r immediately put some beans in his mouth. At once, his ears were filled with a sound: *crunch, crunch, crunch*. The donkeys were chewing. He was chewing. The sound gave Kugen'r a great deal of comfort and support. Kugen'r thought, *Only the living can eat and chew. The dead cannot eat or chew. Although shadows are not dead, they are only shadows made by light. The shadow isn't me, so it cannot eat.* With this thought, Kugen'r suddenly felt elated, suddenly experienced a spiritual satisfaction he had never before enjoyed.

This was the first time that Kugen'r realized that fried beans, in addition to being filling, could also comfort a person and make them happy. The book by Chairman Mao still rested open on his knees. He turned his eyes to the book, to those words he had read thousands of times. The familiar words appeared before his eyes: "All men must die, but death can vary in its significance. The ancient Chinese writer Sima Qian said, 'Though death befalls all men alike, it may be weightier than Mount Tai or lighter than a goose feather.'" To die for the people is weightier than Mount Tai, but to work for the fascists and die for the exploiters and oppressors is lighter than a feather."

Comrade Zhang Side died for the people, so his death is weightier than Mount Tai. Although Old Gimpy Five didn't work for the fascists, he didn't die for the people. He committed suicide—he died for himself, so his death is more insignificant than a goose feather. Of course I will never die for the fascists, nor will I die for myself, but I will die for the people as Chairman Mao instructs. I want my death to be as weighty as Taishan. I'll never put a rope around my neck and hang myself. My father was a revolutionary martyr; I am the son of a martyr; my life belongs to Chairman Mao, to the Party, to the revolution, to the people, crunch, crunch, crunch. . . . *I eat fried beans to sustain my life,* crunch, crunch, *but I sustain my life for the Party, for the revolution, for the people,* crunch, crunch, *for Chairman Mao, and not for myself,* crunch, crunch, *I am a son of the Party,* crunch, crunch, *I am my father,* crunch, crunch, *I am changing the world for my father,* crunch, crunch, crunch. "If we have shortcomings, we are not afraid to have them pointed out and criticized, because we serve the people." Crunch, crunch, crunch, crunch. "*Anyone, no matter who,*" crunch, crunch, crunch, "*may point out our shortcomings." Crunch, crunch. "If he is right, we will correct them."* Crunch, crunch, crunch, *of course I will never die for the fascists, and there is no way I'll die for myself; I want to die for the people as the Chairman instructs. I want my death to be as weighty as Mount Tai. There's no way I'll put a rope around my neck and hang myself; my life is not mine alone—it belongs to the Party, to the revolution, to Chairman Mao, my father,* crunch, crunch, crunch. *He doesn't think I dare. This afternoon, the way he looked at me under the earthen precipice told me. He doesn't think I dare. He's entirely mistaken. He might be right if I were doing this for myself, but I'm doing it for the revolution! They don't think I dare. Returning to the village from the embankment today, he gave me the same look—he thinks that I won't do anything on account of Old Gimpy Five's suicide. He's wrong. He might be right if I were do-ing it for myself, but I'm doing it for the people, for my courage and strength are unlimited. I will do it so that everyone can see. The dead may not be able to do it. This shadow on the wall can't do it, but I can! I'll keep doing it! I'm a materialist. Chairman Mao says, "Thoroughgoing materialists are fearless." I am a thoroughgoing materialist with nothing to fear!* Crunch, crunch, crunch.

The wind blew in and the shadow surged forward and just as suddenly collapsed. Then everything was shrouded in darkness. Kugen'r was covered with goose bumps. Kugen'r thought, *I am a materialist, I have nothing to fear.*

Someone shouted, Kugen'r!

Kugen'r could see nothing. He again thought, *I am a materialist....*

Once again the voice shouted, Kugen'r!

Kugen'r thought, *I have nothing to fear....*

That voice now seemed tinged with fear. Kugen'r, are you there or not? Kugen'r, why don't you say something? Why don't you light a lamp? Kugen'r, what's wrong with you? Are you dead too, Kugen'r?

Kugen'r thought, *I am a materialist. I haven't died, the dead do not fear, I have nothing to fear. . . .*

That voice was now tearful. Kugen'r, Kugen'r, stop scaring me. Is anything wrong? You're scaring the heck out of me. . . .

Kugen'r finally discerned that the person crying outside the door was Nuanyu. Kugen'r thought, *I am a materialist.* Kugen'r felt for the matches and lit the lamp.

Kugen'r said, Nuanyu, it's so late, what is it?

Still crying, Nuanyu said, Fucking Kugen'r, watching over the dead in the dark, you scared the hell out of me. I thought you were dead too.

Kugen'r watched as Nuanyu entered carrying two bowls filled with delicious-smelling hot mutton dumplings. Kugen'r suddenly felt hungry. This time he really was hungry. He salivated as his stomach growled.

Kugen'r said, Nuanyu?

Nuanayu said, These are the dumplings I made for the team to handle Uncle Gimpy's funeral. You are watching over Uncle Gimpy, so you should have some dumplings. This bowl I brought over especially to offer to Uncle Gimpy. When she finished speaking, she placed a bowl for Kugen'r on the windowsill and carried the other bowl into the room. She placed the bowl at the head of the *kang*, knelt, and said, Uncle Gimpy, these are the dumplings from the team for your funeral. Uncle Chuandeng and the others had some; you have some too. As she spoke, tears rolled down her face.

Kugen'r looked at the kneeling silhouette and said, Idealist.

Nuanyu stood up and said, Kugen'r, are they good?

Kugen'r said, I haven't tried them yet. Kugen'r pointed to the head of the *kang* and said, Nuanyu, that's nothing but feudal superstition, it's idealism.

Nuanyu said, Us common folk don't worry about such things as superstition. How can someone die and offerings not be made? I don't know what that "ism" of yours is; anyway, a person must have a good heart. Without a heart a person is nothing more than an animal, right?

Kugen'r said, You have no idea what I am talking about.

Nuanyu lifted the door curtain and said, You don't have to understand. If you spend too much time trying, your dumplings will get cold.

Nuanyu lowered the door curtain. The waft of air created as the door curtain fell once again extinguished the lamp. Kugen'r was again shrouded in icy darkness. He could hear the donkeys eating noisily. Once again he salivated and his stomach growled. The sound of Uncle Chuandeng's saw could really be heard coming from the temple of the Earth God, *ha-la, ha-la, ha-la*. Kugen'r again felt for the matches and relit the lamp. That real shadow and that very real corpse appeared once again.

Kugen'r thought, *I am a materialist, I have nothing to fear. Zhao Yingjie is also a thoroughgoing materialist.*

48

Stunted Flats has been empty since Uncle Gimpy died. Stunted Flats has been totally empty since Uncle Gimpy died. He was hanging from a beam, but I couldn't see his face, just his back. I really regret not having spent more time with him last night, spent more time talking with him. He was hanging from a beam, hanging from a rope above his head. He really looked like a skin hung on the wall, with nothing inside—no bones, no flesh, no heart, no eyes, no mouth, no Uncle Gimpy, just an empty skin hanging there, empty, empty, empty like a kite. It was the same that time. That time we buried my brother; I got married; my mom, dad, brother, and sister all left, leading away a small donkey with a sack of corn on its back. I saw them to the earthen cliff just outside the village and said, Mom, Dad, I'll say good-bye here. Don't bother to come and see me later, and don't tell my brothers or sisters to come and see me. And don't send a letter asking about me. I don't want to know anything or see anything. Here is where I am, and I'm not going anywhere else. . . . Someday, I'll die here. They cried. I told them not to cry. They left. *A winding path of yellow earth, far and long. Blue sky, yellow earth. They are far away over there. I am here. Like a kite, drifting farther and farther, ever higher into the emptiness. So empty it's as if there is nothing under the sky, everything inside and outside is empty. Tell me why people live. If you were the only person left on earth with food to eat, something to drink, clothes to wear, a place to live, and a place to sit, if you had everything and didn't have to worry about anything, would you still want to live if you were the only person alive on earth? No one*

would care for you and you'd have no one to care for. Would life still be
worth living? If a person had nothing to do or think, would she still be
a human being? If a person couldn't do anything or think anything,
would she still be a human being? How would such a person live? All
the people who cared for me have left, gone home. All the people
I cared for have died and are buried in the yellow earth. Every day,
I cooked at home for those two kids; every day, I took food to
them. What would I do if I didn't take food to them? I took food to
them for three days and three nights. On the third night, holding
a bowl, I saw Uncle Gimpy squatting under my window. I said,
Uncle Gimpy, why aren't you at home asleep? Uncle Gimpy said,
Nuanyu, don't take any food to the graves. I said, Why aren't you
at home asleep? Can't you see it's nearly light? Uncle Gimpy said,
Nuanyu, I've been keeping watch here for the last three nights. I
said, Aren't you tired, Uncle Gimpy? Uncle Gimpy said, Nuanyu,
I'm afraid something might happen to you. How can someone eat
after they're dead, Nuanyu? Think about it. Little Cui and your
little brother are both dead. How can they eat? Suddenly it was all
clear. I sat on the threshold and began to cry. Then I thought of
how all those who cared for me and all those I cared for were
dead. I was all alone. My heart was empty. I had no one, no one, I
was all alone. I pressed against his chest and sobbed. I said, Uncle
Gimpy, Uncle Gimpy, I really want to become deformed, the
same as all of you. I'm lonely as hell. Uncle Gimpy sighed and
said, Cry if you feel like it. Have a good cry. I cried. I cried, I cried,
I cried. I really wanted to die. Those who cared for me and those I
cared for are all gone, leaving me all alone here to cry, cry, and
have no one hear me. Why do I go on living? Uncle Gimpy said,
You really make people worry about you; you really make people
feel sorry for you. I cried, I cried, I cried, I cried, Wa, wa, wa. . . .

Uncle Gimpy said, You really make people worry about you; you really make people sorry for you. . . . Uncle Gimpy cared for me; I pressed against his chest and cried for one who cared for me. I cried. I cried. I cried. I cried . . . I cried, never thinking that this day would come when I would be bringing dumplings to Uncle Gimpy. He hanged himself from a beam in the stable with an old hemp rope, like a skin nailed to the wall. The skin was empty, no bones, no flesh, no heart, no eyes, no Uncle Gimpy, just like an empty skin hanging there, empty, empty, empty as a kite. *Yellow earth, blue sky. They are far away over there. I am here. It's like a kite, drifting farther and farther, ever higher into the emptiness. . . . Yellow earth, blue sky. They're far away over there. I am here. . . .* I placed the dumplings at the head of the *kang*, never having dreamed that the day would come when I would be offering dumplings to Uncle Gimpy. How can someone eat after they're dead, Nuanyu? Think about it. Now Uncle Gimpy is dead. Uncle Gimpy can't eat either. I placed the dumplings for Uncle Gimpy at the head of the *kang* and said, These are the dumplings I made for the team to handle Uncle Gimpy's funeral. Uncle Chuandeng and the others had some; you have some too. Uncle Gimpy said, How can someone eat after they're dead, Nuanyu? Think about it. Every day at home I cooked for those two kids; every day I took food to them, for three days and three nights in a row. If I didn't take food to them, why go on living? Kugen'r simply doesn't understand this. Kugen'r isn't ordinary folks. He just doesn't understand the affairs of ordinary folks. Sitting under a lamp, holding a book in his hands, he just didn't understand what I was thinking when I carried the dumplings over. If there was no one else on earth save Kugen'r and his book, he could go on living. Kugen'r has no dad, Kugen'r has no mom, Kugen'r has no kids,

Kugen'r has no one who cares for him, Kugen'r has no one he cares for. If only one Kugen'r remained on earth, have no fear, there'd still be a Kugen'r, who'd, as usual, read his book and talk his reasons, who'd go on being Kugen'r. Tianzhu asked me what I agreed to with him. Everything and nothing. Tianzhu said, Has Stunted Flats treated you badly? Stunted Flats has not treated me badly. I stay here willingly. Erniu said, You're such a nice person, so why do you want to live in this village of cripples? A healthy person like me lives here because I have to. It's not because it's good or pretty here, or it's worth living here, it's because I have to live here. I must be only too willing—those who cared for me and those I cared for all remain here, are all buried here. Where would I go? Tell me. But I never thought Uncle Gimpy would die, I never thought there would be a day when Uncle Gimpy didn't eat. Stunted Flats has been empty since Uncle Gimpy died. Stunted Flats has been totally empty since Uncle Gimpy died. There's no one who cares for me. There's no one I care for. *Yellow earth, blue sky. They're far away over there. I'm here. Yellow earth . . . blue sky . . . they're far away over there. . . . I'm here. . . .*

49

I had to talk to someone. If I kept this bottled up inside me, I'd go crazy for sure. I entered the courtyard, the cave, and sat on the *kang*. I could smell them. I smelled. On the *kang* were a newly made quilted cotton jacket and pants—black on the outside with white lining, and finely stitched. The buttons and button loops were twisted tight and firm. Cloth shoes with newly stitched-on soles lay next to the clothes. There were also shoe lasts, black as well as firm and rigid. Everything was ready. Well made and made quickly. Sitting next to the lamp, I could smell them. I smelled. It smelled good. *She's a good woman. Uncle Gimpy is really lucky. The day I die, I'm afraid I won't have the luck to have a set of clothes like this to wear, and I'm afraid I won't have Uncle Gimpy's luck.* The cave glowed warmly in the light of the lamp. It smelled like new clothes in the cave, like mutton dumplings, and like her. I could smell it all. It smelled good, real good. *She's a good woman.* I heard someone at the courtyard gate. I heard Blackie run toward the gate. I heard her footsteps. She opened the door, lifted the door curtain, and looked up. She saw me. *She's a good woman. Why did I dream of her and Lanzi together?*

She said, Someone sitting here without uttering a word is enough to scare a person to death.

I said, It's an act. I've stayed overnight here more than once. What are you scared of?

She pulled a long face and said, Tianzhu! What day is this? And here you are still talking so improperly!

That year, I was only seven. How could she be together with me and Lanzi? I said, Look, you're angry again. Why are you so angry with a bunch of cripples like us? How come I never see you get angry with the great director? Huh?

She said, If you're so afraid of me, why do you come to my place? Why are you so shameless?

I pulled Lanzi toward me and said, Lanzi, don't move. Then I knelt and drank her milk. I drank a lot of Lanzi's milk, but how could she be standing behind? I laughed and said, If a cripple can't be shameless, who can? The folks of Stunted Flats are born shameless.

She said, Tianzhu, don't argue with me. What is it you really want today?

She followed behind me and I said, Aren't you thirsty? Don't you want some of Lanzi's milk? She said, No. I've got so much milk of my own and no place for it. I said, I'm not arguing; I just want to drink your milk.

She said, Tianzhu, more nonsense, get the heck out of here!

The sun sizzled on the back of my head. I said, I'll drink your milk. She said, No. I laughed and said, When I was seven I drank a lot of Lanzi's milk. Now I want to drink yours.

She said, Tianzhu, are you nuts today or what? What's all this crazy stuff you're talking?

The sun was silent. That year, when I was seven, I don't know where she was, she hadn't been born yet. But how could I dream of her and Lanzi together? I didn't laugh. I said, Nuanyu, I have to speak to you about something, and if I don't, I'll go crazy for sure.

She said, Is it about Uncle Gimpy?

I said, Yes. How did you know?

She said, Hurry and say what you have to say. I don't know anything. What about Uncle Gimpy?

I said, This morning Kugen'r took me to Uncle Gimpy's place, but Uncle Gimpy didn't say anything. Kugen'r wanted him to talk about you and him. Uncle Gimpy refused to say anything. Not a word. Who would have thought he would hang himself? What is this all about? Uncle Gimpy said he couldn't bully a woman, and said no more. He refused to say anything. Who would have thought he would hang himself? But from the start this had nothing to do with you and Uncle Gimpy; Kugen'r and I were out to get Liu. Who would have thought that he would hang himself? If I'd known this would happen, I never would have gone to see him! Am I crazy?

She didn't say a word. She cried. Tears ran from both her eyes.

Her two breasts flowed the same way. After she buried Little Cui, I went to see her. She agreed. She said, Tianzhu, don't worry, I'm not going anywhere, I'm going to die in Stunted Flats. Even if you don't record high work points for me, don't carry water for me or chop firewood, I agree. I won't leave. I said, That's not right. We have to give credit and treat people right. We all have to take care of you. She laughed. I laughed. Later she began to cry. As soon as she started crying, her breasts moved and the front of her shirt was all wet, her milk soaked through her shirt in two places. She sat on the *kang.* I pressed her close to me and said, You see, you see. . . . I helped her open her clothes and saw her two white breasts. I knelt before her—those two breasts were enough for me. I grew up drinking Lanzi's milk but never drank my mom's. Those two breasts were enough for me. I cried and said, Nuanyu, Nuanyu, Nuanyu, I'm kneeling before you, all of us men at Stunted Flats kneel before you—you are our savior. We must treat you well. I cried. She cried too. . . . I pressed her. I said, Nuanyu, don't cry. Say something.

She kept crying. After crying enough, she said, I knew there was something, I knew there was something, I knew that Uncle Gimpy had to have a reason to hang himself. Uncle Gimpy died for me, Uncle Gimpy was muddleheaded. What's the point of dying for such shameless goods as me? What's the point? Uncle Gimpy, Uncle Gimpy, why were you so muddleheaded? Ah, hai-hai-hai . . . Uncle Gimpy . . . you, you . . . ah, hai-hai-hai . . .

Now I regretted it. I knew it was bad. I knew I'd made a mess of things. I shook her and said Nuanyu, Nuanyu, NuanyuNuanyu, NuanyuNuanyu. . . .

She ignored me. She just cried. Cried. She didn't cry when her little brother died. She just cried. She just cried.

How could I dream of being with her when I was seven? The year I turned seven, I came out of the woods, leading Lanzi. The sun sizzled on the back of my head. Nuanyu followed behind me. I saw Huatou in the courtyard after the Japs had cut off his legs. I saw my grandpa, disemboweled by the Japs, strung up on the sacred tree at the entrance of the village. In Ugly Baby's courtyard I saw all the women naked. Ugly Baby's grandpa banged the gong and cried, The Japs are here, it's a disaster, don't think of suicide. If you all kill yourselves, who will have babies for us at Stunted Flats? Ah, hai-hai-hai-hai. . . .

I said, Nuanyu, Nuanyu, don't cry, you'll make yourself sick. If something were to happen to you, the men of Stunted Flats would be finished!

She ignored me. She just cried and cried and cried.

I remembered there was something else I had to say to her. I said, Nuanyu, Nuanyu, you didn't agree to anything with Director Liu, did you? If you did, what will become of the men at Stunted Flats? Say something.

She ignored me. She just cried and cried and cried.

Where was she when I was seven? She hadn't been fucking born! Why was she born so late? Why was I born so early? Fuck it all to hell.

50

Master looked at the lid. Master looked at the lid again. Master sighed and put down the lid. Master didn't scold me. Master didn't beat me. Angry, Master squatted. The fire for the glue pot had gone out a while ago, and there was nothing left but a pile of white ashes. The sky was just beginning to get light. The lamp on the left column was out of oil. The lamp on the right column was out of oil. Both lamps had gone out, and the stage was cold and dark. Master didn't scold me. Master didn't beat me. Master just squatted on the ground, trembling with anger.

I said, Master . . .

Again I said, Master . . .

The stage was cold and dark. I joined my master in trembling.

Master said, Erniu, a person has a face, a tree its bark. Tell me, do you think the coffin can be called a coffin if we use that lid?

I said, Master . . .

Master said, Erniu, a person only dies once. Uncle Gimpy will die only this one time and you and I, master and apprentice, made his coffin. Is this coffin we made adequate? Tell me, do you think we have done right by him? It's impossible to fix it, to compensate him, to apologize, to make it over again! You're impossible! A person can't die a second time!

I said, Master . . .

Master said, Erniu, I've built coffins for people my entire life. I don't know how many people have been laid to rest in the coffins I built. I've never had anyone refuse and say no. Everyone says that they would be fortunate to die before me. This is the first time that your master has ever built a substandard coffin. The reputation of a lifetime! Erniu! Erniu!

I cried and said, Master, beat me! Scold me! I really don't know how I could have messed it up so badly.

Master said, Erniu, if I beat you or scold you, the lid is still cockeyed. If I beat you or scold you, Uncle Gimpy can't die a second time for you. If I beat you or scold you, the wood is still ruined. If I beat you or scold you, your master can't start all over again. Erniu, do you think your master can begin his life again? Is that possible? Can't you see even with two lanterns hanging there? Are you blind? Are you so stupid you couldn't see that it was cockeyed?

I cried and said, I'm not blind. I can see. I was just afraid that you'd be angry when you saw that the wood was the wrong side out. I thought I could plane it smooth and never thought it would become so thin. Hit me! Scold me! I can't go on living unless you beat and scold me! Master!

Master said, Erniu, I did everything else tonight and asked you to make only the lid. The lid is a little more difficult to make, and I wanted to give you some practice. If you never practice, when will you ever learn?

Still crying, I said, Master, beat me! Scold me!

Master was still squatting and trembling. Master said, Erniu, the master is the master and the apprentice the apprentice. Wherever I might go, I can't say that this lid was made by you and not by me. The master is the master and the apprentice the apprentice. Erniu, your master doesn't want to beat you or scold you. Your master only wants to lie down in this coffin and have you nail down the lid. Lying in the coffin with the lid nailed on, your master won't hear anything or see anything. He'll just be at peace.

On the stage, I knelt before my master and said, Master, nail me inside! Nail me inside! I'm the one who ruined the coffin! I'm the one who ruined it!

Master didn't move. Master was still squatting and trembling.

Master said, Little Five, Little Five, I, Li Chuandeng, must apologize to you for the rest of my life.

I watched my master kneel and kowtow to the coffin several times.

I ran over and knelt in front of my master. Crying, I said, Uncle Gimpy, Uncle Gimpy, it was me who ruined your coffin. I'm the one who ruined it, me. . . . I kowtow to you, I kneel before you, I'm sorry, Uncle Gimpy. . . .

The lanterns were out. The sky was light. Master was kneeling. And I was kneeling.

51

My heart froze when I looked at it. I broke out into a cold sweat. Why did I have such confidence in him? Why didn't I keep an eye on things? I was blind. *Can that be called a coffin with that lid? Can Little Five be laid to rest in that thing? Is that what's called craftsmanship?* The master is the master and the apprentice the apprentice. Such an apprentice is just a chip off the old block. But it's a master like me who is to blame. I've done this my whole life, my whole life! Starting with my apprenticeship at fifteen, I've done this for fifty years! A whole life, fifty years, ruined by this one lid. I was blind, blind, blind! Little Five, Little Five, I'm sorry. I'll be sorry the rest of my life. I've done you wrong, Little Five. I, Li Chuandeng, have lost face and am a disappointment. I, Li Chuandeng, have had my failure; I've gone to Mai City as a failure. But why, Little Five, of all people, did I have to fail you? A hero who meets failure, who makes his journey to Mai City, can sing and the picture looks good. Now I've dragged you, who are such a sad person, along with me. It's heartbreaking. I've never wronged a soul in all my life. I'm so sorry now. Little Five, I can get down on my knees before you, but I can't make it up to you. I can kowtow to you, but I can't make it up to you. A person lives their whole life and dies only once. Little Five, you only lived half your life and you died, hanged yourself. But I, Li Chuandeng, let such a sad person as you lie in this thing that by rights can't be called a coffin. Little Five, oh, Little Five, I, Li Chuandeng, have harmed you so that you can't even die like a human being. I kneel to you, I kowtow to you, but I can't make it up to you.

52

A group of men shouted as they hoisted the coffin. Poplar wood. It's not heavy. But still the group shouted, One, two, lift, go, go!

Tianzhu swore, You fuckers, walk steady! Humi, put a little more into it, damn it—can't you see it's all going crooked on your end?

The coffin swayed as it rose from the stage. Wood shavings and chips were heard underfoot—*hua-la, hua-la, hua-la*. Each person had a strip of red cloth affixed to his chest; the strips of red cloth all swayed as well. A bunch of cripples shouldered the white coffin on the stage. *Hua-la, hua-la*—it sounded as if they were crossing a river. It's said that when a person dies they have to cross a river—this was Uncle Gimpy's river.

Tianzhu swore again, Humi, didn't you fucking hear me? Put more into it!

Peng-deng, the coffin hit one of the columns.

Tianzhu shouted, I told you to keep it steady. Damn it, can't any of you hear me? If you break the coffin, which one of you has more wood to make it up to Uncle Gimpy? Keep it steady.

Ancestors. Nothing but swearing and more swearing. One lousy commune member and he can swear at whomever he damn well pleases. Uncle Chuandeng and Erniu followed behind. Uncle Chuandeng looked downcast and didn't say a word. Uncle Chuandeng was upset about the thin lid. Erniu was also silent. Erniu glanced from Uncle Chuandeng to the coffin. Erniu wished it could be him inside the coffin. No one was dressed in funeral garb, there were no banners or weeping mourners, just the *hua-la, hua-la* underfoot, just Tianzhu swearing up a storm. *Uncle Gimpy, you are pitiful. Sadly, you lived as a poor unmarried man. At times like these, it's good to have a son or close relative.* The group carried the coffin down off the stage and out of the grounds of the Earth God's Temple, turned at the pediment, curved around the stone roller to the courtyard of the stable. A flatbed cart was ready there. Erhei was harnessed and standing there, flicking his tail. Seeing the coffin approach, Erhei brayed. Uncle Gimpy had nothing except Erhei. *I'm even worse off because I don't even have an Erhei, though I do have a Sack, who has to look after that fucker called Dad. Sack doesn't know he's not Third Dog. Sack is Sack. Sack doesn't know that he's not his dad; the one he is always swearing at is his dad. But Sack doesn't know. Sack doesn't know a damned thing. Sack doesn't know why he's called Sack, nor does Sack know why the earth is filled with fluttering leaves,* hua-la, hua-la, hua-la. *The earth is filled with fluttering leaves,* hua-la, hua-la, hua-la, *and not shavings on the stage,* hua-la, hua-la, hua-la. Placing the coffin on the cart, the group stood in the courtyard with their hands folded, not uttering a word.

Tianzhu said, Ugly Baby, let's carry Uncle Gimpy out.

Ugly Baby didn't say a word and followed Tianzhu into the stable. The group of men stood around, hands folded, saying nothing. Then out came Uncle Gimpy. He was dressed in black cotton clothes and wearing black shoes, all made by Nuanyu. They put Uncle Gimpy in the coffin, then put the lid on, and then they too stood to one side, arms folded. Uncle Chuandeng and Erniu stepped forward with an axe and nails. Uncle Chuandeng and Erniu nailed on the lid.

Hammering in a nail, Uncle Chuandeng said, Little Five, watch the nails.

Hammering in a nail, Erniu said, Uncle Gimpy, watch the nails.

No one is dressed in funeral garb, there are no banners or weeping mourners. Just the flashing axes, just the beat of the axes on the coffin. The day I die, no one will dress in funeral garb, nor will there be banners and weeping mourners. I have Sack, but he doesn't know he's my son. Sack still thinks he's his son. Actually he's not his, but mine. Knowing and not knowing are the same. But I know that when I die, Sack won't wear funeral garb for me, hang a banner, or weep in mourning. That's because Sack doesn't know I'm his father. I'm even sadder than Uncle Gimpy—he had Erhei, and Erhei cries for him. Sack doesn't know who I am. He only knows that I'm Humi. He doesn't know that Humi is his dad. Knowing is knowing; not knowing is not knowing. Sack, Sack, Dad is so pitiful. Sad Uncle Gimpy, sad Erhei, sad me, and sad you, do you understand? Sack, Sack, my son! My Erhei, my Erhei, your father will sooner or later let you know! I'm not afraid of not earning work points the rest of my life; I'm not afraid of going hungry the rest of my life. Your dad just wants you to know who your real dad is. In the blink of an eye, the hammering stopped and all was silent. *The coffin is nailed shut. Uncle Gimpy is nailed inside. Uncle Gimpy can't get out.* Hua-la, hua-la, the wood shavings made no sound. *Uncle Gimpy has crossed his river. That river was too deep and too long. Once across, Uncle Gimpy won't be coming back. Uncle Gimpy left Erhei on this side of the river, left Sack and me on this side of the river, left Nuanyu on this side of the river, and left Stunted Flats on this side of the river. But the day will come when Humi must cross that river, Sack must cross that river, Nuanyu must cross that river, that fucker must cross the river, and all of Stunted Flats must cross that river. I wonder which side of the river has more people, this side or that side. I wonder which side of the river has more villages, this side or that side. I wonder which side of the river is larger, this side or that side. How big is it on the other side? People cross every day, every year, and have crossed for thousands of years. Why isn't it full? How can there still be space? People die every day, every year, and they've done so for thousands of years. Is there no end to death on this side? Why so many villages on this side? Is it because all the living have died and all the dead have returned to life? Living and dying, living and dying, living and dying for thousands of years, dying and living for thousands of years. Is it life or death? Death or life? There's no damned way for anyone to be certain. Uncle Gimpy is certain; Uncle Gimpy has reached the end. The coffin was nailed shut and Uncle Gimpy was nailed inside and can't get out. Uncle Gimpy can't say a word.* No one was saying anything. Everyone was standing around with arms folded, saying nothing. *A bunch of cripples standing on this side of the river, in a courtyard, around a coffin, silent. Standing around Uncle Gimpy's boat for crossing the river.*

Tianzhu said, Let's go. Let's have some noodles.

Everyone walked out of the courtyard, around the pediment at the Earth God Temple, and to the gate of Nuanyu's courtyard. Before they even entered, they could smell the mutton. Fuck! It smelled good! Their cheeks tingled and saliva flowed between their teeth. *People on this side of the river have mutton noodles to eat. I wonder if the people on the other side of the river are cooking noodles for Uncle Gimpy.*

53

I knew there was something wrong with him. He hadn't been quite right since yesterday. He swore at everyone on his way back from the embankment, he swore when he went to dig the grave at Fifteen Mu, and now he was swearing as he carried the coffin.

There was something wrong with him. What was it? What was he so upset about? He hadn't been quite right since yesterday.

He said, Ugly Baby, let's carry Uncle Gimpy out.

I followed him into the stable, into the room. Uncle Gimpy was lying there dressed in new clothes, making people feel uncomfortable. It was like the one lying there wasn't Uncle Gimpy, more like a bridegroom. I'd never seen such a change in my whole life. It was so new it seemed wrong.

He got up on the *kang* and said, Ugly Baby, I'll lift his head, you get his feet.

I moved toward his feet.

Lifting Uncle Gimpy's head, he cried and said, Uncle Gimpy, this is such a sad life. Fuck it all to hell! Why is it so damned hard to live out one's life? Fuck it all to hell!

I tried to boost his spirits a bit and said, Tianzhu . . . Tianzhu . . . what are you crying for? Huh?

Lifting Uncle Gimpy's head, he said, Ugly Baby, you don't understand. I'm the one who did him in!

I said, Tianzhu, Tianzhu, what kind of nonsense is that? Uncle Gimpy hanged himself.

He said, Ugly Baby, you don't understand. Yesterday morning Kugen'r and I went to see Uncle Gimpy. Kugen'r wanted him to tell about his relationship with Nuanyu. Kugen'r wants to get Commune Head Liu, and I'm afraid he wants to take Nuanyu away. That sissy Kugen'r just wants some accomplishments. But Uncle Gimpy wouldn't talk. He refused to talk. Who knew he would hang himself? If I'd known he was going to hang himself, do you think I would have visited him? Fuck it all to hell.

Uncle Gimpy was lying there dressed in new clothes, so new that he looked like a bridegroom.

I pressed him and said, Tianzhu, I could see since last night that you haven't been quite right. I knew you had to be mixed up in something here. Don't cry. And don't speculate. It's hard enough understanding the living. Do you think you can explain the dead? Uncle Gimpy took a rope and hanged himself. What makes you think you know why? If you guys hadn't come yesterday morning, who's to say that he wouldn't have still hanged himself? If you were to come tomorrow morning, would he have hanged himself tomorrow morning? If you guys never showed up, does that mean he never would have hanged himself? When a person decides to die, do they come to that decision one morning? Have you ever died? You talk about death as if it were so simple and clear. Have you become an immortal?

Still crying, he said, Fuck it all to hell! It would better if I'd hanged myself! At least that way I could wear the new clothes made by Nuanyu. It would be better for you guys to bury me today! Why is it so damned hard for a man to live out his life? Ugly Baby, why is it so hard? Life is so hard, but what other way is there? It would be better just to learn from Uncle Gimpy. Close your eyes and have all your problems vanish!

I said, What kind of fucking nonsense are you talking? If you die, who'll take care of those four dogs of yours? That's the easy way out. Close your eyes and rest. Who'll take care of your kids? You don't want to take care of your own flesh and blood? No? Are you human? Or are you a beast? Okay, don't cry. Crying, you're more like a woman confined after childbirth. Are you acting like a man? A team leader? We grew up bare-assed together, but I don't know what you can do. Pick him up, there's a bunch of guys waiting outside. Pick him up, make it snappy; otherwise, Uncle Gimpy will have every right to scold us.

We picked him up. We carried the new Uncle Gimpy to his new coffin. We placed the new Uncle Gimpy in his new coffin. We watched as Uncle Chuandeng and his apprentice ran in new nails, *ding-dong, ding-dong, ding-dong,* nailing the coffin shut. Then there was nothing left to see. The cold, dry sun shone on the white coffin. When a man lives his life, lives it till it's stale, then he puts on a new suit of clothes, lies down in his coffin, and dies.

What is it to enjoy a life of ease and comfort? What is a life of suffering? Is the way Uncle Gimpy lived and died suffering? Is the way Tianzhu and I live a life of ease and comfort? Yes? No? It's hard to say. Perhaps Uncle Gimpy knows, knows only too well. He hanged himself with a rope and died. Humi is right—if you haven't reached the end, you don't know what it is. When you get to the end and you know what it is, you're damned well dead and gone too. When you're fucking dead, you've got no way to tell others about it. To tell the truth, let the Old Man in Heaven take care of it all. People have got no business in it.

The cold, dry sun shone on the white coffin. Shining as Tianzhu cried his eyes red. *Fucking Tianzhu is usually pretty foul-mouthed, and swears at the drop of a hat, but he can cry like a woman confined after childbirth when something's happened.* When he was seven years old, I was seven too. When he was seven, the Japs disemboweled his grandpa, cut the legs off Huatou, and stripped the village women naked in our courtyard. It scared the shit out of him, and he cried all summer long. That day I wasn't caught by the Japs; my grandpa hid me in the flour chest. If I'd been caught by the Japs that day, it would have meant my life, and I wouldn't be here today to carry Uncle Gimpy.

Uncle Gimpy is wearing a new suit of clothes and is laid out in a new coffin. Nobody knows why he did it. Nobody knows if he was happy or sad.

54

She gave me a lot of noodles. She just looked at me. It made me uncomfortable. What was she looking at? Hadn't she ever seen anyone eat before?

She called me, Erniu, Erniu.

I looked up at her over the edge of my bowl.

She said, Erniu, take your time, there's no need to rush.

I lowered my head. I ate. The cave was filled with a slurping sound. Heads lowered, the whole group was eating noodles. All eyes were fixed on the noodles. No one was looking at me. No one was looking at her.

She said, Erniu, take your time. When you finish, I'll give you some more.

I lowered my head and ate for all I was worth. I gulped down a whole bowl of mutton noodles in no time flat. The noodles were no good because there was elm-bark flour in them. Too much elm-bark flour, made everything red. The noodles were no good, but the mutton was. I ate for all I was worth. I wolfed down a whole bowl in no time flat. Holding my bowl, I stood beside the stove. I looked at her and held the bowl out to her.

I said, More noodles.

She ladled in the noodles and more meat. She heaped it up. She said, Erniu, this is your third bowl. Take your time, there's no hurry. When you finish, I'll give you some more.

Laofan shouted, Look! Look! Look at Erniu's bowl. That's real mutton noodles.

Tianzhu cursed, Laofan! Mutton noodles aren't enough to stuff your fucking mouth! The noodles are the team's and so is the meat, it's no concern of yours!

Laofan smiled. Laofan said, I'm not concerned about the noodles or the meat. I'm saying that someone cares for Erniu and that no one cares about me. Just look at everyone's bowls.

Everyone looked at my bowl. Master looked too. They made me feel really uncomfortable. I put down my bowl. I wouldn't eat.

She said, Erniu, have you eaten your fill? If you're full, don't eat any more. You don't want to burst.

I wasn't full, but I put down my bowl and wouldn't eat.

Tianzhu said, Nuanyu! What are you doing? Erniu and Uncle Chuandeng worked all night, why are you telling them not to eat? Erniu, don't listen to her. Eat up!

I didn't want to pick up my bowl. I said, I won't eat.

Tianzhu's eyes were wide open. Nuanyu! Look at you.

Then she cried. She said, Erniu, Erniu, I'm not stopping you from eating. My little brother died from overeating noodles that year. If I had kept an eye on him and been more careful and not allowed him to eat that last bowl of noodles, Huniu wouldn't have died and would have been able to go home. If Huniu had gone home, he'd be able to come and see me.

The cave full of people was silent. No one ate. They just watched her cry. I did the same. Now I knew why she was always looking at me. Now I knew why such a healthy person like her had to stay in a crippled place like Stunted Flats.

She cried for a while, then looked up and smiled. She wiped the tears from her eyes and said, Everybody eat up. Don't let me disturb you. Honestly. She said, Erniu, hurry and eat, don't listen to my nonsense.

I picked up my bowl. Everyone else did the same. Once again the cave was filled with the sound of slurping. There was too much elm-bark flour in the noodles. The noodles were bad, but the meat was good. Everyone wolfed it down.

Laofan said, Fuck, this is good!

Humi said, It is good. If it weren't for Uncle Gimpy, we wouldn't be eating these mutton noodles.

Lafan said, Well, why don't you go hang yourself too? Then we can have some more mutton noodles!

Humi smiled and said, If one person hangs himself each day, we'll have mutton noodles every day, and one less person to eat them each day. In less than a month, there won't be anyone left in Stunted Flats to butcher the sheep, or anyone to eat noodles. Laofan, are you thinking to rush to the front to eat noodles, or you want to be the very last? You can't butcher a sheep, so how will you eat noodles?

All the men in the cave laughed, coarse and hearty.

Laofan shoved a piece of mutton into his mouth and said, Fucking Humi! You always have to have the last word, and you won't give up till you've nailed someone's ass. If you don't have the last word, you just go and keep your mouth shut.

Humi laughed and said, That's right. But don't I nail every mother's ass to start with, huh?

All the men in the cave laughed, even more coarsely and crudely. Holding their chopsticks, someone raised their hand and said, Humi fucking nailed it again.

Tianzhu scolded them again, Had enough to eat? Had enough to eat? You just keep going on and on with this nonsense, you can just put down your damned bowls.

She stood by the stove, looking at me and smiling. She said, Erniu, why do you look so much like my little brother? Why do you look so much like Huniu? You even eat the same way.

I buried my head in my bowl. The noodles were bad, but the meat was good. I slurped away. *I'm not her little brother. I'm not Huniu. I'm Erniu.* I was in the middle of eating noodles. The noodles were bad, but the meat was good. *I'm not her little brother— I'm still alive.*

55

The green one comes out the green one is on the cart close to me the green one is on the cart the green one is close to me

56

The two of us sat on the ground, close to the courtyard wall. Blackie sat facing us. Occasionally he stuck out his red tongue, rolling his tongue over his mouth, over his mouth. I knew Blackie smelled it. Second Dog also stuck out his tongue and ran it over his lips.

Second Dog said, Brother, I smell it—it smells so good!

I said, I smell it too.

Second Dog said, Brother, why don't we go in and have a look?

I said, Second Dog, you have no shame. I suppose you want to go in and get something to eat?

Second Dog said, Brother, I don't want anything to eat, I just want to look.

I said, And see what? Everyone eating mutton noodles? What's to see, standing there to one side? I can see you're itching for it.

Second Dog said, Brother, why do people eat mutton noodles when someone dies? Last time, when Ugly Baby's granny died, people ate mutton noodles, and now that Uncle Gimpy is dead, people are eating them again. If Dad died, would we have to eat mutton noodles?

I said, Second Dog! You're fucking talking nonsense. If Dad heard you, he'd beat the heck out of us.

Blackie stuck out his tongue and rolled it over his lips. Second Dog stuck out his tongue and ran it over his lips. Blackie got up and headed for the drainage hole. Second Dog pulled on Blackie's tail.

Second Dog said, Blackie! You have no shame. You just want to go in and get something to eat.

Blackie yelped. Second Dog didn't let go. Blackie yelped several times before backing out of the drainage hole. The three of us sat at the bottom of the courtyard wall facing one another.

Second Dog said, Blackie, don't be in such a hurry. The day I die, you can have mutton noodles. I won't keep you sitting to one side just smelling them. Second Dog looked me and said, Brother, I'll let him have some, but not the grownups. Am I right?

I said, Second Dog, quit talking nonsense. If you die, there won't be any more you. If you don't exist, how can you eat mutton noodles?

Second Dog looked at me. Second Dog stuck out his tongue and said, Brother, I can smell it.

57

When he exhaled, I felt her breath on my face, warm and gentle. I turned to look at him. Looking at him made me want to cry, but I controlled myself. I knew he wanted to cry. I spoke to him, trying to hearten him.

I said, Erhei, we're in no hurry, take your time, it's still early. Anyway, he's gone.

He blinked and blinked. He wanted to cry.

I said, Erhei, let's not cry. We still have to pull the cart. Uncle Gimpy is on your cart.

He turned her head toward me. His breath was warm on my face, making my eyes tingle.

I said, Erhei, Uncle Gimpy only has this short stretch left; let's take our time to let Uncle Gimpy see and hear a bit more. The sun today is so nice. He left before we did, and this time he's certainly gone down in the valley.

He blinked and blinked. He wanted to cry. I wanted to cry too, but I controlled myself.

There was no need to go down in the valley to reach Fifteen Mu. Just turn at the sacred tree at the entrance to the village and head due north on the road of yellow earth—wide and long like a river—stretching out over the plains. I didn't want them to see my face. I led him, walking in front of them. He hadn't eaten or drunk since Uncle Gimpy hanged himself yesterday. He'd been upset and digging at the ground. His mind was like a bright mirror—he understood everything, everything was clear, you couldn't hide anything from him. Yesterday, a group dug the grave, Uncle Chuandeng built the coffin, Nuanyu made new clothes for him; today we ate mutton noodles, and now we were on our way to bury him. Even so, we couldn't hide the truth from him. No one was dressed in mourning, there were no banners, no one broke any dishes, no one was weeping in mourning, there was no sign, but you couldn't fool him. A road of yellow earth— long and wide like a river—stretched across the plains. After thirty years, a daughter-in-law becomes an old lady; in thirty years a road becomes a river. Uncle Gimpy had come to the end and didn't want to go on any longer. At the end of the river was Fifteen Mu, at the south end of which was a north-facing bank, at the foot of which the grave was dug, a hole seven *chi* deep, waist high, and the stones to stop up the hole were already placed in order by the grave. Uncle Gimpy was rushing headlong there. When he hanged himself from that beam, he saw and thought about this river and that piece of land at the end of it, that piece of land called Fifteen Mu. Fifteen Mu belonged to Uncle Gimpy a long, long time ago. Uncle Gimpy thought of nothing else but being buried there on his own land. He understood everything, you couldn't hide anything from him.

He blinked and blinked. He wanted to cry. I felt like crying. But I didn't want that bunch to see me, so I controlled myself.

I said, Erhei, let's take our time to let Uncle Gimpy see and hear a bit more. Uncle Gimpy only has this short stretch left. Yesterday morning Kugen'r and I went there, but today, I was at his place putting my thumbprint on that pile of documents; I really did. He asked me if I agreed, and I said, Yes. So he took my thumbprint. Each of us made our mark in red. Two people left two red marks. Then he took the documents and left. He walks faster than us; by now he must be leaving the valley.

He understood. He shook his head. I knew he understood and that he was still sad. I knew that I had affixed my thumbprint and he'd gone off to the county seat. But Uncle Gimpy was still dead. He'd come back from the county seat. I could still have some mutton noodles. But Uncle Gimpy couldn't. He was dead and gone. Death is just the end of the road. He was dead and wouldn't come back. Even if the river were wider and straighter, there'd still be no coming back.

I couldn't cry. If I cried, he'd cry. They would see the two of us crying. I said, Erhei, I know for the rest of my life I'll feel that I wronged Uncle Gimpy, and you too. But he walks fast and we walk slowly, and so I must explain things to you. He walks fast, so he prepared two pairs of shoes and a pack of dried food, and said he would walk all night to get to the county seat by tomorrow morning. He said, "The Red Army doesn't fear the difficulties of a long march." He said he wasn't afraid of the 165 *li*, nor was he afraid of the fucker who wanted to take Nuanyu away. We walk slowly because only this stretch remains for Uncle Gimpy. We want him to see and hear a bit more. When we get to the end, there won't be anything left for him to see or hear.

People are all different. Some people hear and see nothing their entire life. It's not that a person can't hear or see; he just doesn't listen or look. He lives his whole life, he lives a hundred years, but it's in vain. But he is different. He doesn't need to listen or to see. He sees and hears everything. He lives one day, and it's the same as a whole life. He lives one day, and it's a thousand years. I stroked his neck. I stroked her for a lifetime, I stroked him for a thousand years.

I said, Erhei, Erhei, you're Uncle Gimpy's child, you were his good fortune. Look, before Uncle Gimpy left, he gave you a new rope. He was thinking of you before he left. Uncle Gimpy loved you for a reason. With you, Uncle Gimpy had everything.

He snorted. I could feel his breath on my face, warm and gentle. I felt like crying. But I didn't want anyone to see me. Uncle Gimpy ought to have been leading him; Uncle Gimpy should have felt his breath on his face, warm and gentle. But now it was warm and gentle on my face. Uncle Gimpy couldn't stand up here. He was lying in the coffin built by Uncle Chuandeng, lying in the cart being pulled by Erhei. Uncle Chuandeng nailed the coffin shut. It was the end of the road of yellow earth. The grave had already been dug at Fifteen Mu. The rocks to seal up the grave were all prepared. The grave hole was at the edge of Fifteen Mu, on the north-facing slope, waist high, seven *chi* deep.

Once he was laid in that hole, it'd all be over, nothing left, with no thought of ever coming back. He'd be back from the county seat, I'd have a chance to eat mutton noodles. But Uncle Gimpy wouldn't be coming back, ever.

I said, Erhei, I know you don't believe me. But I have to tell you. I'm different from that fucker. I'm different from him too. Holding up those documents, he said, "We have come together for a common revolutionary goal." I said, No, we're different. I said, You are determined to get credit for some accomplishments. I'm afraid that that fucker will take Nuanyu away. He said, The general direction of the revolution is the same. I said, The general direction is different. You're going east to the county seat; I'm going north to Fifteen Mu. He said, Rest assured that Zhao Yingjie and I will see this through to the end. I said I didn't know who the fuck Zhao Yingjie was, and all I wanted to do was handle my own business, and I couldn't count on anyone else. He didn't say anything. He just left. He left alone and walked very fast, with nothing but a book bag on his back. We are walking slowly because we are pulling a cart and on the cart is Uncle Gimpy. It's because this is the final stretch for Uncle Gimpy. Erhei, I know you don't believe me now. If you don't believe me, you don't believe me, it can't be helped. But I have to tell you. I'm different from that fucker. I'm different from him too.

He was so close you could feel his warmth and gentleness; he was so close you could smell his scent. I had no idea how many times Uncle Gimpy must have stroked his warm form or how many times he must have smelled his scent. He was shiny, black, and clean. That was because Uncle Gimpy swept up and cleaned up after him. He was Uncle Gimpy's darling. Uncle Gimpy loved him. Having lived his whole life with love in it, he did not live in vain. This life of his was better than to have lived a thousand years with no love. Am I not right? Erhei, what do you say?

I stroked his neck, stroked him forever. I said, Erhei, Erhei, I know you are angry with me, I know you hate me, I know I harmed Uncle Gimpy. But I have to explain it to you. He left early today. He walks faster than us. He took two pairs of shoes, a book bag with dry food, the documents with our thumbprints on them, and a letter of introduction with a big red seal on it. He said with that letter and the big red seal on it, he could enter the county seat and find a high official there and bring about that fucker's downfall. With that fucker's downfall, he could avenge Uncle Gimpy, and the fucker would have to give up trying to take Nuanyu away. If that fucker had not brought those documents, nothing would have happened at Stunted Flats. He walks fast and said he wasn't afraid of those 165 *li*. We walk slowly, because this is the final stretch for Uncle Gimpy.

A road of yellow earth across the open plains. A road of yellow earth, wide and long, like a river. A bunch of cripples walked on the road. There were no funeral banners. No one was dressed in mourning. No one was crying. Nothing. Just a donkey cart, a coffin, and a bunch of cripples. I felt like crying, but I couldn't. I didn't want the others to see me crying. I didn't want him to see me cry either. Leading him, I felt his breath on my face.

I said, Erhei, let's take our time. This is the final stretch for Uncle Gimpy.

He blinked and blinked. He didn't look at me.

58

We arrived. We arrived on foot. A bunch of us stood in a circle waiting for Tianzhu to speak. Glum, Tianzhu was silent. Glum and silent, Tianzhu walked the whole way without paying attention to anyone. Tianzhu pulled out a pack of Greenleaf cigarettes, tore it open, clutched all twenty cigarettes in his hand, and then threw away the empty pack. Everyone was watching him. Everyone knew he was going to pass out the cigarettes.

Tianzhu said, Each person take one cigarette.

No one said a word. Each person stepped forward to take a cigarette. Everyone smoked. Smoke rose from the ends of the cigarettes. We waited till everyone was finished smoking.

Tianzhu said, Lift it up.

No one said a word. Everyone stepped forward to lend a hand. Everyone lifted.

Tianzhu said, Fuckers, hold it steady!

The shining white coffin rose off the cart. Then it was placed on the ground. The harvested field was empty. It had been plowed. It had been harrowed. It was flat and open. It was neat and clean. The freshly dug tomb looked like a black, bottomless eye, open in the ground at Fifteen Mu; it looked like a toothless black maw, gaping in the ground at Fifteen Mu. The sun was just beginning its descent, casting the shadows of the cripples on the ground. The people were pretty stunted. The shadows were long. It looked like a bunch of ghosts flitting across the ground at Fifteen Mu.

Tianzhu again said, Lift.

Everyone stretched out a hand and lifted.

Tianzhu swore at me, Humi, put your fucking back into it. Can't you see the coffin is going off crooked in your direction? Do you think Uncle Gimpy is going into his tomb crooked?

I exerted a little more strength. The coffin straightened. Uncle Gimpy faced that black eye, that black, gaping mouth. Head facing out. Feet facing in. Erhei dug at the ground again. *Dig, thud, dig, thud, dig, thud,* numbing the hearts of everyone. Erhei made a drum of the ground at Fifteen Mu. *Thud, thud, thud,* numbing everyone's hearts.

Tianzhu said, In with it.

The group moved forward. Facing in. Backs facing out. *Thud, thud, thud, thud.* The more the coffin entered, the darker it got.

Tianzhu said, Steady, put it down, slowly.

The group put Uncle Gimpy down. Head facing out. Feet facing in. Face upward. *Thud, thud.* It was all yellow earth save for the bright opening. *Thud.* Soon the hole would be sealed, the eye closed, the mouth shut. *Thud.* Only Uncle Gimpy would remain inside, slowly turning to earth. *Thud, thud.* Slowly becoming identical to the yellow earth he was buried in. *Thud, thud, thud.* Turning to earth, to nothing. *Thud.* Then something will sprout from the earth. *Thud.* Grass, trees, flowers, birds, bugs, crops, *thud, thud.* Something will grow from there and everything will be right. *Thud.* There'll be everything, everything. *Thud, thud.*

Tianzhu said, Let's go.

Everyone stepped back. Outside you could see the sky, the land, the sun, Erhei, the others, and yourself. Erhei was still digging, digging, *thud, dig, thud.* The sun has been hanging in the sky looking down on the world below, on the people below, for who knows how many thousands or tens of thousands of years.

It has been looking ever since Pan Gu separated the heavens and the earth with a giant axe. *Dig, thud.* It was always looking down, always looking down. *Thud, thud.* Seeing that there was nothing in the world, that it was wrong. *Thud.* Looking again at the world. There was everything on this side of the river; everything was right. *Thud.* There's nothing on this side of the river, everything is wrong. *Thud.* The sun damned well knows if this side of the river is bigger, or that side of the river. *Thud.* The sun damned well knows if on this side of the river there is nothing and it's small or if there is everything and it's big. *Thud, thud.*

Only the sun has watched thousands, tens of thousands of years of living and dying, only it has seen it all clearly. *Thud, thud.* Who knows if it has told the moon or not? Who knows if it has discussed it with the moon or not? *Thud, thud.* I'm sure it must have told it and discussed it. If it didn't say something or discuss it, wouldn't it be bored to death after thousands or tens of thousands of years? *Thud, thud.* And besides, it's like when something happens at home and the men don't discuss it with the women, but don't they always have to discuss things? *Thud, thud.*

I fuck his ancestors! Even the sun has a wife, an old lady. Uncle Gimpy and I have unfortunately always been motherfucking poor unmarried men. Fuck it all to hell! Thud, thud. *That fucker Tianzhu has seen through this whole matter. Tianzhu fucks it all to hell.* Thud, thud. *Erhei has seen through the whole matter as well. Erhei digs, thuds, digs. Erhei wants to dig his way across the river to the other side to find Uncle Gimpy.* Dig, thud, dig, thud, dig, thud.

Tianzhu took a basket out of the cart and took some stuff out of it. Tianzhu went back into the tomb. Tianzhu sprinkled the five kinds of grain around the coffin, placed several coins at the head of the coffin, and lit several sticks of incense, which he placed in a bowl in front of the coffin. He also lit a sesame-oil lamp. The lamp, once lit, illumined Uncle Gimpy's coffin and the tomb.

Tianzhu said, Humi, Tiecheng, Laofan, you three seal up the opening. Tianzhu looked at Erhei and said, Erhei, stop digging. Rest assured, we gave Uncle Gimpy a good funeral, nothing that would make him feel uncomfortable.

Me, Tiecheng, and Laofan piled up the stones, leaving a space the size of a fist in the piled wall. Tianzhu then picked up a purple-footed red rooster and walked over. Tianzhu shoved its head in the hole, and then slapped its rear end twice to push it through.

Tianzhu asked, Did all the gravediggers come out?

Standing behind him, we all said Yes.

Tianzhu said, Seal it up.

We sealed up that last hole. We also set three flagstones in front of the tomb to serve as a table. Tianzhu took out some spirit money and lit it. The flames turned the yellow paper into black ash. Something became nothing.

Tianzhu looked at Uncle Gimpy's tomb. He looked at the paper turning to black ashes. Tianzhu said, Uncle Gimpy, we apologize for not preparing anything for you. You have no children. You have no relatives. There's no one to dress in mourning for you, cry for you, spread a funeral banner for you, or break a basin for you. Nothing. We're sorry, Uncle Gimpy. Uncle Gimpy, we won't see you anymore, we have nothing for you. You liked to listen to me sing, so I'll sing a little for you, Uncle Gimpy.

Tianzhu sang:

> Wearing a crown of jade and phoenix bun,
> Dressed in royal robes of eight treasures,
> The brocade gown tight at the waist,
> Jade ornaments tinkle as you move with ladylike steps.
> Tianzhu cried,
> My grandfather celebrates his birthday this morning.
> Hundreds of officials, civil and military, pay their respects.
> Innumerable fine carriages and horses arrive at the mansion,
> Music of flute and pipe last all the way till dawn.

Tianzhu knelt to Uncle Gimpy and said, Uncle Gimpy, Uncle Gimpy, and then broke down in fitful sobbing.

Someone said, Tianzhu! Tianzhu! Don't cry. Something'll happen. Look—Erhei is running away!

Tianzhu didn't listen. Tianzhu kept on crying.

I turned and looked and saw that Erhei had run a long way off. Erhei pulled the cart by himself, running along that road of yellow earth, farther and farther and farther until he disappeared from sight.

Erhei went crazy!

59

The green one is gone the green one is gone the green one is gone I want to find the green one I want to find the green one I want to find the green one

60

But the Second Platoon Leader was waiting for me at the commune. I had been wanting to make it clear to her, I had been wanting to make it clear to her. The moment I saw him, I knew he was behind it. His damned shoes were worn out. But she didn't seem to hear a word I said. She said she wanted to tell me one thing. Was this any motherfucking time for that? The Second Platoon Leader was waiting for me at the commune and you want to tell me one thing. Tell me what it is you wanted to say?

That woman! Damn, you'll never guess in a million motherfucking years what that woman really wants. I had to tell her. I knew there was no point in trying to be motherfucking clear with a woman. How did she know that the Second Platoon Leader was waiting for me at the commune? Doesn't she know who the Second Platoon Leader is? The Second Platoon Leader is Zhou, who is head of a section. Doesn't she know that? There's no point in thinking you can make it motherfucking clear to her. I handed the card to her. I said, Nuanyu, here! She said, What's this? There was no damned way to make it clear to her. I said, Haven't you been waiting for the sun to rise in the west? This is the divorce certificate you asked for! She looked at me, cried, and said, Why are you such a fool? There's something I have to tell you. I knew I hadn't been clear with her. But I had to try. The Second Platoon Leader was waiting for me at the commune. He was standing next to the Second Platoon Leader, a book bag on his back, his shoes falling apart. I knew he was behind it all. I knew something was going to happen. Before they entered, I was lying on my bed counting sparrows, one, two, three, four, five . . . the sparrows were hopping in the courtyard, but I couldn't get a motherfucking clear count. I started again, one, two, three . . . when they came in. He stood there, his shoes falling apart. I knew something was going to happen. If something else happened, I'd still have to deal with it. My woman was there, how could I not go? I said, Nuanyu, don't cry. Listen to me. I'm not the Commune Head Liu I once was. I'm now just Liu Changsheng. I'm just me. Liu Changsheng wasn't always called Liu Changsheng. Liu Changsheng was originally called No Good Liu. I wore a pair of worn-out shoes, threadbare cotton clothes, and stood facing Political Commissar Wang, who asked me, What's your name? I said, No Good Liu. Political Commissar Wang smiled and said, That's not a good name; henceforth, you'll be called Liu Changsheng. The revolutionary troops want always to be victorious in battle. From then on, I followed Political Commissar Wang, my name was Liu Changsheng, and later I became Director Liu. In those days, the Second Platoon Leader was just the Second Platoon Leader. That was before Zhou, the current Director of the

Organizational Department of the County Political Committee, was the Second Platoon Leader. She was still crying. Crying, she said, Why are you such a fool? I still have something to tell you. I knew there is damn well no motherfucking point in trying to make things clear to a woman. I said, Nuanyu, first hear what I have to say, the Second Platoon Leader is Director Zhou, who conveyed to me the directive of the County Party Committee and the County Revolutionary Committee, that I am no longer commune head. They made him the motherfucking acting head. Him and his worn-out shoes—they made him the damned acting head in my place! They said I'm the model case for purifying class ranks in the county. They set up a special group to examine me and ordered me to the county seat for study and to undergo investigation. Fortunately it was Second Platoon Leader who announced it. Second Platoon Leader was my old commanding officer when I was with the County Regiment. I said, Second Platoon Leader, the marriage laws stipulate that a person must be eighteen to get married. I'm thirty-eight and I can't divorce and remarry? Is divorcing and remarrying the new trend in class struggle? If divorcing and remarrying has become the new trend in class struggle, then how many motherfucking new trends are there in all of China? Second Platoon Leader said, Comrade Liu, you are a Party member and must obey the organization, that's a principle. I said, Nuanyu, do you understand? I'm a Party member and have devoted my entire life to the revolution. I'm a Party member, so I obey the organization, that's a principle. Principles are principles. A principle is something you can't violate, even if it means death. I obey the organization, I obey principles, but I'm not the person I used to be. I'm not Commune Head Liu;

I have to attend a special study group. I'm not Commune Head Liu; I'm now Liu Changsheng, I'm not anything, I'm just myself. But principles are principles. A principle is something you can't violate, even if it means death. A principle is something that can't be violated by my former self or my present self. If I violate a principle, I'm not a Party member and my lifetime devotion to the revolution has been for nothing. Do you understand that or not? I had to come and tell you, right? My woman is here, had I any other motherfucking choice but to come?

She said, I understand. You've told me the truth, now I want to tell you the truth too. I wanted to tell you a long time ago, but you didn't let me. She said, I've got a baby in my belly, and it's not yours.

Damn, you'll never guess in a million motherfucking years what that woman really wants. You want a woman heart and soul and with heart and soul you think she is yours. Then she tells you she is pregnant and that the motherfucking thing isn't yours! Then I said, Whose woman are you? Whose kid is it? Damn it, why didn't you fucking tell me earlier? Who else have you slept with besides me? How many guys have you slept with? Tell me. Damn it, why didn't you fucking tell me earlier? I'm not the commune head; I'm not the person I used to be. You're pregnant, so you're not who you once were. I even gave up being commune head for you and damn it, you tell me you're going to have a baby and it isn't mine. What the hell is this? Who are you really? Whose woman are you? Speak up!

She looked at me and said, I wanted to tell you, but you wouldn't let me. I don't know who you are, but I know who I am. My name is Qin Nuanyu and I came to Stunted Flats as a beggar fleeing famine. My little brother died here. My baby girl Little

Cui died here. I'm no one's woman, I'm my own woman. My baby is no one's but mine. She looked at me again and said, I have one more thing to say that I haven't told you. I'm leaving tomorrow. I'm leaving Stunted Flats tomorrow and going home. I'm my father's. I'm my mother's. I'm my own. I belong at my old home.

I know motherfucking well you better not expect a woman to understand. You'll never figure out what she wants in a million years!

61

The people who cared for me have all left, all gone home. The people I cared for have all died and are buried in the yellow earth.

A large road of yellow earth twists and turns, long and far. Yellow earth, blue sky; I'm over here, they are over there. Blue sky, yellow earth; they are over there, I am over here.

62

There was nothing on the dirt road. Just the two of us.

He was dragging along behind me. He said, Brother, did you really see it?

I said, Yes.

He said, What if you saw wrong?

I said, I'm not mistaken.

He said, What did Dad give Uncle Gimpy?

I said, Crackers, a box of crackers.

He said, What happens if you saw wrong?

I said, Do you want to eat or not?

He pouted and said, Brother, there's nothing here. Let's go home. If Dad finds out we ate Uncle Gimpy's crackers, he'll beat the heck out of us.

I said, I'm going, even if you don't.

We walked. There was nothing on the dirt road. Just the two of us.

He twisted his face and started to cry. He's as ugly as she is when he cries. I clenched my fists and saw Erhei.

I said, Second Dog, Second Dog, don't cry. Erhei's coming.

Second Dog stopped crying. Second Dog saw Erhei. Erhei was pulling a cart all alone, walking from a distance. There was nothing on the dirt road. Just Erhei walking, and the two of us.

Second Dog said, Brother, wasn't Erhei lost? How did he get back? Does he know that there's a box of crackers with Uncle Gimpy?

I said, Second Dog, you're right; Erhei wasn't gone, he has been looking for Uncle Gimpy.

There was nothing on the dirt road. Just Erhei walking, and the two of us. The adults all said Erhei was gone, Erhei was crazy. They said he went to Gula Valley, Nanliu Village, Wuren Flats, that he went to the eastern slope and Laoling Gully. They said Erhei would go around the world and never come back, not back to Stunted Flats.

Second Dog said, Brother, didn't all the adults say Erhei was gone, that he was crazy? But isn't Erhei okay?

There was nothing on the dirt road, just Erhei walking over there.

I said, Second Dog, the adults don't know Erhei. All they know is how to take a whip and beat Erhei. They're all bad. They know nothing but beating Erhei with a whip.

He said, Brother, let's not use a whip, let's not hit Erhei, let's not be bad people.

I said, Right. Second Dog, remember, we won't be bad people when we grow up, we won't hit Erhei.

He said, Brother, we're all cripples, so we won't grow up.

There was nothing on the dirt road, just Erhei getting closer and closer.

He said, Brother, have Erhei give us a ride.

The two of us shouted, Erhei! Erhei! Erhei!

There was nothing on the dirt road. Erhei lifted his head. Erhei saw me and Second Dog. There was nothing on the dirt road, just Erhei getting closer and closer.

He laughed and said, Brother, let's get on the cart.

Erhei just took off with the two of us. There was nothing on the dirt road. Just me, Second Dog, and Erhei.

He said, Brother, where are we going?

I said, I don't know. We're going with Erhei.

He said, Brother, Erhei's not going back to the village, Erhei's turning.

I said, I can see, Second Dog.

He said, Brother, let's not go home, let's just go with Erhei!

I said, Okay, we'll go with Erhei.

He laughed and said, Brother, Erhei runs really fast!

63

Wu-wa-wa-wa-wa. . . . Ah-wa-wa-wa-wa. . . . Ya-wa-wa-wa-wa. . . .

WEATHERHEAD BOOKS ON ASIA

WEATHERHEAD EAST ASIAN INSTITUTE, COLUMBIA UNIVERSITY

(*continued from page ii*)

Qian Zhongshu, *Humans, Beasts, and Ghosts: Stories and Essays*, edited by
Christopher G. Rea, translated by Dennis T. Hu, Nathan K. Mao, Yiran Mao,
Christopher G. Rea, and Philip F. Williams (2011)
Dung Kai-cheung, *Atlas: The Archaeology of an Imaginary City*,
translated by Dung Kai-cheung, Anders Hansson, and Bonnie S. McDougall (2012)
O Chŏnghŭi, *River of Fire and Other Stories*, translated by Bruce Fulton
and Ju-Chan Fulton (2012)

HISTORY, SOCIETY, AND CULTURE
Carol Gluck, Editor

Takeuchi Yoshimi, *What Is Modernity? Writings of Takeuchi Yoshimi*,
edited and translated, with an introduction, by Richard F. Calichman (2005)
Contemporary Japanese Thought, edited and translated by Richard F. Calichman (2005)
Overcoming Modernity, edited and translated by Richard F. Calichman (2008)
Natsume Sōseki, Theory of Literature *and Other Critical Writings*, edited and
translated by Michael Bourdaghs, Atsuko Ueda, and Joseph A. Murphy (2009)
Kojin Karatani, *History and Repetition*, edited by Seiji M. Lippit (2012)

GPSR Authorized Representative: Easy Access System Europe, Mustamäe tee 50, 10621 Tallinn, Estonia, gpsr.requests@easproject.com